VOLUME TWO

EVERNIGHT PUBLISHING ®

www.evernightpublishing.com

MONSTERS OF NEW YORK

Copyright© 2025

ISBN: 978-0-3695-1288-8

Cover Artist: Jay Aheer

Editor: Lisa Petrocelli

ALL RIGHTS RESERVED

VOLUME TWO

Monsters of New York is a sizzling paranormal romance series where passion collides with danger in the heart of the city that never sleeps. Each book introduces a new, irresistible shifter—each with its own dark secrets and primal desires. From wolves and bears to elusive creatures lurking in the shadows, these powerful beings navigate love, loyalty, and mystery in a world filled with human and supernatural monsters.

Set against the backdrop of New York's vibrant streets and hidden corners, every romance is an unforgettable journey where forbidden love and heated encounters could be the death of them—or the one thing that saves them. With danger always just around the corner, the shifters must face not only the threats of their own kind but the intense pull of a love that could change everything.

Uncover the secrets, feel the heat, and discover if love can tame the wildest beasts in Monsters of New York.

VOLUME TWO

CONSUMED BY THE BROTHERS

Monsters of New York

Lila Fox

Copyright © 2025

Chapter One

Jenna set her tray on the bar and waited until Thomas, the bartender, came to get her order. She looked around the room at all the different people. That night, The Gin Room was busier than she'd seen so far. Although, she'd only been in New York a few weeks and at this job for only one.

She'd left her home in Nebraska because she'd always had this need to roam. Her parents didn't understand this and were afraid of her living in such a big city, but they hadn't been able to change her mind.

Jenna had been apprehensive too, but it helped when a high school friend, Nicole, decided to move with her. They'd saved up for a year, working several jobs to earn money. When they moved to the city, they were shocked to find that everything was at least triple the price of what it had been at home.

They'd been lucky to find an apartment that was being subleased to them for eight months, plenty of time to find a permanent apartment. It had fallen onto their laps when she started working at The Gin Room. Her friend, Nicole, had gotten a job as a secretary for a small business, and she seemed to love it.

The apartment's owner had to make an emergency trip back to Argentina for a sick family member and had already been gone, but they'd been able to FaceTime.

"What can I get you, Doll?"

Jenna looked up at the bartender, Thomas. "Here's an order."

He looked at the sheet and nodded. "I'll be right back."

Jenna learned not to get too friendly with any man because they took it as a come-on. The realization had happened quickly after starting the job.

The Gin Room was the first place to hire her. She wasn't thrilled working in a bar. Although upscale, it still had a few dirtbags who wouldn't leave her alone. Most of them were harmless, but there was one in particular that scared the living shit out of her—Westen Payne.

She could tell right off the bat that he was dangerous and someone to stay away from—as far away as she could, being in the same building. From what she'd been told, he was the head of an organization, one that stole, killed, and took whatever they wanted. At the moment, he wanted her.

He'd come in every night since she'd worked there and sat in the same booth, and his eyes followed her everywhere. It always sent chills up her spine and made her stomach cramp painfully. If she hadn't needed the job so much, she would have been gone. Now, she was trying to look for another job.

"Here you go, Doll," Thomas said.

She arranged the glasses on the tray. "Thank you."

"You're welcome. A piece of advice, stay away from Payne. He's bad news."

She looked up at Thomas and nodded. "I saw that immediately, but he won't leave me alone."

"Did Mick put Melanie in his section?" Thomas asked.

"Yes. Thank God. But that doesn't keep him from staring at me all night."

Thomas sighed. "I'll talk to Mick. Maybe he can put you on days?"

"I already asked." The moment she felt threatened by Payne, she went to Mick, her night manager, and asked to change, but until one of the girls left, he didn't have an opening. He promised to keep an eye on the situation, but the man was always busy.

"Do the best you can."

Jenna nodded. "Thanks, Thomas."

Jenna went about her business for the rest of the night. She exhaled in relief when she saw a man come into the bar, go directly to Payne, bend down, and say something. Immediately, the group of men stood and walked out.

Please, God. Keep him as far away from me as possible.

Several nights passed without the scary man, and it was so peaceful she actually enjoyed herself.

Jenna waved as she walked out the front door of the bar. She was happy. She knew she made a lot of money with tips, and her feet didn't ache like they had at the beginning.

It always surprised her how many people were

still awake when she left the bar around one a.m. or later. All kinds of people, from the very rich with their fancy clothes, purses, and jewelry to the homeless who, if they were lucky, might have a cart to haul their worldly possessions but usually only had a few bags. She could have stood against the building for an hour just watching the river of people, but she was tired and wanted to see her friend, Nicole.

She started walking to the bus stop, where she'd grab a ride that would drop her a few blocks from her apartment.

Jenna was jostled enough that she hit the building hard with her shoulder, and she gasped. Dammit. She looked around and couldn't see who might have done it. Hell, anyone could have pushed it, and she'd never know.

She moved to get out of the stream of people and rotated her arm to see if it was injured or just bruised. A sound to the right had her turning, only to have a hand cover her mouth and an arm with an unbreakable grip wrap around her waist and start pulling her into the alley. She frantically fought and prayed that someone—anyone—would see and come to her aid. But the people just walked past.

Jenna could see the black dots in her vision and knew she was seconds away from passing out. Her lungs contracted when she was suddenly dropped onto the ground. She thought she would have a chance now to escape, but the scene before her was unlike anything she'd seen before.

A big cat that looked amazingly like a cougar and … God, was that a wolf? … were tearing into each other. This couldn't be happening. This was New York City. They didn't have wild animals roaming the streets.

Something slammed against the back of her head. Bright spurts of light and pain that radiated through her body made her breath catch, and then nothing.

Her last thought was that she wondered which would be better—a wild animal or a man to deal with. She passed out before she got her answer.

VOLUME TWO

Chapter Two

Rowan had been following a scent for days, but he'd been so busy he hadn't had the time to investigate as much as he wanted. But the allure of the scent grew stronger, and it was getting more difficult to leave alone.

Rowan loved the city because it was easy to hide with a million people around. But at the moment, all the individuals made it hard for him to find what he was looking for. It had either been good luck or the universe helping, when he found the scent and now knew it was a female at the same time she was being mugged. He instantly shifted into his wolf when he realized the mugger was, in fact, another shifter.

The woman had fallen to the dirty, slimy pavement, and he could do nothing about it until he took care of her attacker. He wanted to grin when the man shifted to a cougar because it would not take him long to put the thing down, and wolf shifters fought better than cats in the city.

It didn't take long for the cat to run away. It was either escape with wounds that would eventually heal, or die in the same muck he'd dropped the woman.

He waited until the cat disappeared before pulling on the clothing, which he had mostly ripped apart by shifting, but it was better than nothing.

Rowan picked the woman off the ground and started back toward one of the apartments his pack had in case one of them needed it. At the back of what looked like a dilapidated building, he pressed his finger to the hidden lock and heard it disengage. He took her up a flight of stairs, into one of the bedrooms, and gently laid her on the mattress. He took a step back to see the thing that had been driving him crazy the last few days.

The scent he chased was one he'd heard about from mated pack members. It was a clean fruity smell with the hint of feminine arousal that had permeated every pore in his body and made his cock harder than it had ever been. He could have fucked anyone, it didn't need to be their mate. In all the years he'd been on earth when he thought he'd never find her, he used the females in the pack but knew it wouldn't be the same as fucking his mate.

He'd found his mate, or rather, his and his brother's mate, and he never thought it would happen. They both had given up on finding her, especially in a big city or in another state.

Rowan took a deep breath and shed the clothes on his body before wrapping a towel around his waist and undressing her. Because he wanted her to be comfortable, and he'd be able to see any injuries she might have. He quickly stripped her. Fuck, she was beautiful in clothing, but her body was a work of art. Everything about her turned him on. It took an amazing amount of strength not to stare down at her for hours, and he covered her with the blanket.

One thought kept intruding in his head. What if his mate was not his brother's? They had always assumed they would share a mate because of the family history, but there was always a chance they wouldn't be the same.

God, it would kill him not to be able to share, and his brother Ben would have to keep looking for himself. But his days were usually filled with whatever the pack needed. He was the alpha of the pack, so he had very little downtime. As his beta, it was his responsibility to protect the pack, so he'd always been able to roam.

The two had talked about their mate a few times, more when they were younger. Now, five decades later, they both figured it would never happen. He knew many pack members who never found their mates. They could have full lives but didn't have the happiness and contentment mated shifters had.

The fact that his brother would never have children who would fall into his place of being the pack's alpha when he was ready bothered them. His brother Ben had been taught from an early age by their father what it took to be the alpha of their pack, and his whole life was spent learning everything he could to be the best leader.

As beta, he'd had to learn a lot too, because there was always a chance, a slim one, that if something happened to Ben, Rowan would have to take over as the alpha. It was something he had no desire to do.

He glanced at her face when he heard a small moan. Her hand came up and touched her head, but her eyes stayed closed. Rowan sat on the mattress by her hip and faced her. He rested his hand on the other side of her torso.

"Hey, Sweetheart," he said.

The woman froze and then blinked her eyes several times before she concentrated on him. Her eyes widened as they scanned his upper body. When her eyes clashed with his, she made a small, panicked sound. He could also feel the fear grow inside of her.

"Easy, Sweetheart. No one here will ever hurt you. I saved you from the mugger that accosted you in the alley. Do you remember that?"

"Yes. I'm not sure it was a mugger, though."

What the hell? "What do you mean?" he asked.

"When I got a good look at the guy, I recognized him from the bar I work at. He's one of Payne's men."

Rowan's brows snapped together. "Payne? As in Westen Payne?"

"Yes. I work at The Gin Room bar, he has taken

an interest in me and he won't leave me alone."

That explains the cougar shifter. Payne's whole group was cat shifters. Fuck, the guy was pure evil and not someone he'd want around his mate.

"I'll deal with Payne. You don't have to worry about him anymore."

The woman looked like she wanted to ask another question but rubbed one of her temples. "My head hurts."

"When the guy dropped you, you hit your head. There's a little goose egg, but it didn't break the skin. How's your vision?" he asked.

She studied the wall behind him. "Good. No double vision."

"Any nausea?"

"No."

"We'll keep our eye on you."

She focused on him. "Who are you?"

"I'm sorry. I'm Rowan Hammond. What's your name?"

"I'm Jenna McDonald."

He smiled down at her. "I wish we had met under better circumstances, but I'm glad I was there to help."

"Thank you. I have a feeling Payne would have liked to hurt me."

"He's evil. That's for sure." Hell, the man was worse than evil. He was a sadist with a black soul.

"Why are you in a towel?" Jenna asked.

"My clothes were dirty from the fight."

"Did you get hurt?"

He smiled. "No, Sweetheart."

He could tell the first moment she noticed she was naked and only a blanket covered her.

"Wait!" she exclaimed.

"Easy. You were filthy, and I had to check for injuries," he told her.

He could tell she was starting to panic. He cupped her face. "Jenna, look at me." He had to repeat himself a few more times before she heard. "I want you to really look at me and tell me what you feel."

Jenna looked confused. "We just met … I don't know you."

"Look into my eyes, Sweetheart."

They stared at each other. The longer she looked, the more relaxed she became. "You feel it, too?" he asked.

"I'm not sure what it is, but for some reason, I'm certain you won't hurt me."

He caressed her cheek with his thumb. "Never. There's so much I want to say, but I can tell you're in pain, so let's get you some aspirin and into a shower."

Rowan started to pull the blanket down, but she grabbed it and held it tightly against her chest.

He sighed. "Hold on."

He walked into the bathroom and grabbed one of the robes. When he got back, he helped her sit up and put her arms in the robe. When it covered her, he pulled the blanket down.

"Let me help," he said and lifted her off the bed to stand on her feet. "How do you feel? Any dizziness?"

"No. I'm good."

He wrapped an arm around her waist and led her to the bathroom. It contained everything she would need because they always kept their hidden apartments fully stocked.

He leaned her against the counter and turned on the shower, making sure the water wasn't too hot. "Do you think you'll need help?"

"Not right now," she said.

Rowan nodded, reluctant to leave her, but he didn't want to push her anymore. "I'll be in the bedroom so I can hear you if you call out."

"Thank you, Rowan."

He cupped her chin. "You're very welcome."

He was shocked at how much strength it took for him to leave her and shut the door. He never wanted anything between them—not even a door.

Chapter Three

Jenna stood under the water as it beat down on her shoulders and back. The hot water soothed any injuries or tight muscles she had, and she knew there had to be a few bruises because of the fight she put up.

She was careful around the bump on her head and scrubbed her hair twice to get all the gunk she had on her from the disgusting alley.

When she finished washing, she turned off the water and wrung it out of her hair before twisting it up in a towel. She grabbed another towel and dried off quickly. She looked through the cabinets until she found lotion and slathered it all over her body, which made her feel more human.

She didn't want to put on the robe she'd been wearing because she could see the grime she'd gotten on it, so she reached for another, making sure the belt was tied securely.

A grimace crossed her face when she got a good look at herself. She could see the scraps on one cheek, and it looked like a bruise on her neck.

She pulled the towel off and combed her hair. She gasped when the comb hit her tender head. It was a small sound but enough for Rowan to burst through the door with a concerned frown on his face.

"What's wrong?" he asked.

"It's nothing. I just accidentally hit the bump on my head."

He nodded. "Is there anything I can do?"

She was starting to shake. "No, I think…"

He was behind her with an arm around her waist when her legs started to sag. "Easy. I've got you. Can I help dry your hair so you can rest?"

"I should be getting home."

He shook his head. "Sweetheart, Payne is going to know where you live. You're not safe until my brother and I take care of him."

God, the thought of having to see the man again made her nauseous. A thought popped into her head. "Oh, my God. My roommate. Will he hurt her?"

"Give me your address, and I'll send someone over to get her. We'll put her in another place until this is resolved."

"Can't we stay together?" she asked.

"No. It will be easier to protect you if you're in different parts of the city," he said.

Jenna didn't really understand but kept quiet. She gave him her address. "Maybe I should call to give her a heads-up. My friend Nicole will fight anyone she doesn't know."

He sat her down on the toilet seat. "Are you okay sitting here for a second?"

She nodded and rested her elbow on the counter for support. She heard him in the bedroom talking to someone, and then he walked back in.

"I've sent one of my men to her. Here." He handed her his phone. "Call her and tell her you're being looked after and that my pack ... I mean, family, will take care of the situation."

Jenna didn't say anything about him calling his people "pack," and called her friend. It rang several times before Nicole's voicemail came on. Jenna called again and got the same thing.

"She's not answering. I'm scared, Rowan. She always answers."

He reached for his phone and made another call. "Go as quickly as you can. Her friend might be in danger."

Rowan set the phone to the side, took out the blow-dryer, and plugged it in. He was careful around the bump, but it was very nice to have someone take care of her now.

"Let's get you back in bed. I changed the sheets and blanket so they're clean."

"Thank you."

Rowan smiled and helped her to her feet. He wrapped an arm around her waist and led her back into the bedroom. He got her situated under the blanket.

"I'm going to shower, but I'll have the phone with me, so I won't miss a call. You just relax. Okay?"

She nodded.

She closed her eyes. She must have dozed because a sound woke her, and she saw Rowan in shorts with wet hair on the phone. She couldn't tell what was being said, if it was good or bad, because his expression stayed blank.

She knew something had happened when he came to her and sat by her hip. "My men got to her in time, but she was beaten. She's not seriously hurt, so they're going to take her to another apartment. They'll bring in a doctor if they think it's necessary."

Oh my God. "How bad?" she asked, wiping the tears from her face.

"She'll have a black eye, bruising, and a few cuts. She doesn't have a head injury like you do, so we don't have to worry about that."

"Did they catch the guy?"

She couldn't decipher his expression, but then he nodded.

"Yes, he's been taken care of," Rowan said.

"The police arrested him?"

Rowan paused. "Yes. He won't be hurting anyone

ever again."

That sounded more ominous than being arrested. There was always a chance the man could get bail, but the tone of his voice made her believe him. She and her friend would never have to deal with at least that guy again. She didn't need to know the whole truth.

"I'd like to talk to her."

He nodded. "Hold on. I'll see if it's possible."

Jenna tried to relax, but she knew she wouldn't feel content until she talked to her friend.

Rowan talked to the person for a moment before handing it to her. "She's groggy but otherwise okay."

She nodded. "Nicole?"

"Hey, Jenna," Nicole said.

"I'm so sorry," Jenna said and started crying.

"Why are you sorry? You didn't do this," Nicole said.

"We think it might be that guy at The Gin Room I told you about. The creepy one," Jenna said.

Nicole exhaled. "Even if it is, it's still not your fault, Jenna."

"Are you in much pain?"

"No. Dillion gave me some awesome painkillers."

Jenna relaxed in relief and smiled when Nicole laughed.

"When will I be able to see you?" Nicole asked.

Jenna looked at Rowan. "When can we see each other?"

Rowan shook his head. "Not right now. Besides the fact you're both injured, we need to track down this bastard, Payne, and get him off the street before I feel okay with you exposed."

Jenna nodded. "Nicole, Rowan said not right now. They want to make sure it's safe for us."

"Yeah, I get that. Am I supposed to stay with

these guys?"

Rowan must have heard her because he nodded.

"Rowan said yes," Jenna told her friend.

Nicole sighed. "Fine. I guess my job is over."

Damn, Nicole really likes that job. "I'm sorry. We'll find another one."

"Tell her that my pa—family—has lived here all our lives, so we know this city like the back of our hands. We also own several businesses. We might be able to find a job for her."

"Nicole, did you hear that?"

"Yes. We'll see what happens."

"Get some rest. We'll talk later," Jenna said. She hung up and handed the phone to Rowan.

She couldn't get over the fact that her friend could have been killed because of her.

Rowan sat down next to her on the mattress. "This is not your fault. You didn't ask for Payne to pay attention to you. The man is a monster. He doesn't care who he hurts."

Jenna sighed. "Thank you. That helps a little."

He smoothed the hair off her face. "Everything will be okay. Just trust me. I know it's a lot to ask since we just met, but please know we have your best interest at heart."

"You keep saying we. Who's the *we*?" she asked.

"It's my brother."

"Will I get to meet him?"

Rowan nodded. "Yes. Soon. He doesn't know about you yet."

That sounded a bit strange, but she was too tired to ask questions.

"Sleep."

"Where will you be?" she asked, suddenly anxious at the thought he'd leave her.

VOLUME TWO

"I'll be right here."

"Okay." She turned to her side and closed her eyes. She'd wait until she woke up to ask the questions she wanted.

Chapter Four

Rowan stared down at Jenna for a long time. Everything about her was perfect so far. Oh, he knew the universe would do this because they were destined to be together, so they had to find each other irresistible.

He walked into the living room and called his brother.

"Hey," Ben answered.

"Hey. I've got some news," Rowan said.

"Okay." Ben waited for a moment. "Tell me."

"I found her," Rowan told him.

"Who?"

"Our mate."

Rowan heard Ben breathing, but his brother stayed silent for a moment. Rowan knew how he felt. They never thought it would happen.

"What if she's just yours?" Ben asked.

"I really don't think the universe would separate us like that. We've known since we were young pups that we would share a mate."

Ben growled. "Fuck. I hope you're right. When can I meet her?"

Rowan went over everything that had happened in the last few hours. He didn't have to hear his brother's fury because he felt the waves of rage through the phone.

"She's okay. Just a little banged up."

"I want to meet her today," Ben said.

Rowan smiled. "I figured. She's asleep right now. I'll get her some clothing and head over after she wakes up."

"I'll send Bishop and a few others to get you here safe," Ben said.

"Have him wait in the back alley. The fewer people that see her, the better," Rowan said.

"You got it. See you soon."

Rowan hung up and went back to bed to stare down at the person, the only one who could truly make him and his brother happy and content. The fact that she could have been taken from him before he ever knew about her sickened him. What if Payne had gotten her? He knew the man would have eventually killed her. He would have never known he and his brother's mate was so fucking close and they had lost her. They would have continued to try to find their mate, but she would have already been gone.

He'd talk to Ben later about the situation, but they needed to get rid of that sick cat before he did any more harm to their pack or even the city. Payne was poison and should be eradicated.

After showering, Rowan walked into the bedroom closet where all kinds of clothing, for women and men, were stored for the pack to use when needed. He pulled out some jeans and a shirt for himself. They had set up every apartment all over the city to protect each member and give them a place to recuperate or just be alone.

After he finished dressing, he pulled out a long skirt and loose shirt to match. He glanced through the shoes and grabbed some sandals for her to wear instead of the dirty tennis shoes she was wearing. Both he and his brother would make sure their mate had everything she needed or wanted.

When he returned to the bedroom, he saw her sitting in the middle of the bed. Since she was so tiny, sitting on the king-size mattress made her look even smaller.

"Hey," he murmured softly, not wanting to startle her.

Her face jerked toward him, and he caught a flash of fear before she recognized who he was.

"Hi," she said.

"How are you feeling?" he asked.

"I have a headache, but nothing I can't handle."

Rowan swore. "Hold on." He walked out but was back with a glass of water and two pills. He sat next to her and helped her take the aspirin he should have given her at the beginning.

"What is this?" she said after she swallowed the last of the water.

"Just painkillers." He lightly ran his fingers over the back of her head where the bump was.

He needed to make her feel better, especially since they were going to meet his brother.

Rowan didn't know how much to tell her. "Baby, I have some clothing for you. Let me help you with it."

Jenna grabbed the blanket when he tried to pull it away.

"You're tired and in pain." He ran his hand up and down her back. "Let me help."

She sat frozen for a moment before she sighed and nodded.

"Good girl." He pulled the blanket away and then untied the belt to the robe and slipped it down her arms. His eyes roamed over the picture she made naked, sitting in front of him with the robe pooled around her waist.

"You're beautiful," he said. He couldn't help reaching out to graze one of her nipples with the back of his fingers.

He was pleased when she gasped, and her body jerked, but the best part was how hard and red her nipple got from just that caress alone.

"Why do I feel so hot and needy right now?" she asked.

He could hear the nervousness in her tone and reached for her hand. "There's a lot we need to talk about, Baby. But I want to be with my brother when you ask the questions. Just know this. Everything is good. There is nothing you have to worry about."

"W-when will we see your brother?" she asked.

"Later today."

Jenna nodded and reached for the shirt. He helped her slide it on and then made her stand beside the bed.

"Step into the skirt, Baby."

Jenna let him slide the skirt up her body and over her hips. Damn, she looked beautiful and so fucking feminine, and her arousal filled the room, making his mouth water and his canines elongate.

"I need my bra," she said when she looked down at herself.

"No. It was ripped, but I gave you a bigger shirt for that reason."

"What about panties?"

He shook his head. "No." They had some in the apartment, but he wasn't going to let her wear any.

It took him more strength than he ever thought to control himself. The wolf in him wanted to mark her so everyone could see, but he also wanted to wait for his brother. He fought to get under control.

"Sit down," he said. When she was on the edge of the mattress, he knelt in front of her and slipped on the sandals.

"Wow," she said and smiled. "How did you get all the right sizes?"

He grinned. "You made it easy. You're so tiny."

"You make me feel that way."

He stood and easily lifted her to her feet. "I want to get some food in you."

She shook her head. "I'm not really hungry right

now."

"Are you still in pain?"

"My head aches but not bad," she said.

He cupped her face in his hands. "I have to kiss you. I need to taste you before we leave. All right?"

Jenna hesitated and then nodded.

Rowan's lips touched hers, and it felt like lights exploded behind his eyelids, and everything around them faded. The emotions were so powerful it should have scared him, but she was his and his brother's mate. Everything they felt now would intensify with time, so he had better get used to it quickly.

Chapter Five

Jenna reached up and grabbed onto his thick wrists as he deepened the hottest kiss she'd ever had. Although her thoughts were scattered after the shock of the first contact, her feelings were also out of control, and she didn't understand why.

If he asked her to lay down and pull up her skirt for him, she would have done it at that moment, and she'd never been like that before in her life.

One of his arms wrapped around her waist to pull her tightly against his body. She felt every muscle in his chest and how hard his cock was as it throbbed against her abdomen. She almost reached for it but stopped when he lifted his head to stare down at her.

"Fuck, Baby. We're going to burn the bed to ashes when we get you onto one."

He said "we" again. Did he expect his brother to be able to touch her, too? It was kind of what he had hinted at, and she didn't know how to ask him about it.

"Come on, before I take you back to bed," he told her and led her out of the bedroom.

She listened as he called someone as they made their way down the stairs.

"I'm bringing her out. Have the men braced for anything."

Jenna stiffened. For a moment, she'd forgotten the danger she was in. But she noticed that as long as she was close to Rowan, she felt safe. As impossible as it sounded, she knew deep inside that he'd never let anything happen to her.

A man at the bottom of the stairs opened the door and then followed them out. Rowan quickly got her into the back of a large SUV, and they drove off in seconds.

She looked over her shoulder to see another SUV like theirs behind them.

Rowan took her hand. "No need to worry. Ben and I just don't want to take any chances with you."

"Ben is your brother?" she asked.

"Yes."

They drove through the streets, and at four o'clock in the morning, she would have thought the streets and sidewalks would be deserted. It seemed New Yorkers like to be out and about at all hours. Fortunately, at that time of day, there was less traffic, so it was easy for them to drive down the streets.

She'd heard the saying that New York is the city that never sleeps, and now she knew it was true.

They pulled up behind another building, and men came out from everywhere to watch over them as they went in. There were a few inside the building until they got to the elevator.

Once inside, Rowan pulled her in front of him, with her back to his front, wrapped his arms around her waist and laid his chin on the top of her head.

"I want you to remember what I said. No harm will ever come to you when you're with us."

She looked up and over her shoulder before she nodded.

Jenna knew that in seconds, she'd meet Rowan's brother, and it would change the rest of her life. She should have been terrified, but instead a certain excitement filled her.

The elevator doors slid open, and her eyes went to the large man across the room. He looked a lot like Rowan, but his facial features were more rugged, and his eyes darker. They were the same size, both tall and bulky with muscles. The only difference she could see was that

Rowan wore jeans and a black t-shirt, while Ben wore nice dress pants and a button-down shirt in a light green color.

She stood frozen, unable to take her eyes off him, while she gripped Rowan's wrists where they pressed against her stomach to hold her against him.

Jenna had been so captivated by this new man, she hadn't realized they were talking about her. When she questioned them, Ben asked her to sit on the sofa. The first touch with Ben had her desire grow. It was like the way Rowan made her feel.

When Rowan sat beside her and took her hand, it helped settle her nerves a bit.

VOLUME TWO

Chapter Six

The elevator door opened, and Ben's breath caught in his throat. His brother had told him of her beauty, but she surpassed what he had expected.

The two came to stand in front of his desk.

"Ben, I'd like you to meet our ... Jenna," Rowan said.

Mate. That was what he wanted to yell from the top of the building. It was a dream he'd wished for since he was a cub. He'd always been told the chances of finding your true mate were not great and to not get his hopes up. It had been hard to do at times, especially when he was around other pack members and their mates.

Ben could see and feel the depth of their love for each other every time, and it always stirred up his emotions. A few times, after spending time with the mated couples, he'd been depressed for days. He would never have shown it and never admitted it to anyone, even his brother.

He realized she was staring at him, and her grip on his brother's wrist was tight. He smelled the air and couldn't detect any fear—just arousal from all three of them and confusion from her.

Ben stood and walked around the desk to stand in front of her. He caught the scent Rowan had been telling him about. His friend, brother, and beta of the pack just hadn't told him how intoxicating and arousing it was.

His eyes roamed over her. She was wearing a dress that reached an inch above her knees. Its light flower design made her look more feminine.

He clutched his hands into fists to prevent himself from reaching for her. He looked toward his beta to see the huge smile on his face. He could tell he was as captivated by her as Rowan was, telling them everything they needed to know. They were both her mates.

Rowan chuckled. "This is perfect."

Ben nodded. "I agree." He felt his canines elongate as his wolf tried to take over, but he held it back, knowing she didn't know what they were yet, and he didn't want to frighten her.

"I smell you on her."

Rowan grinned. "Well, I've been with her for several hours and in close proximity, so that's natural."

"What are you guys talking about?" she asked as she looked back and forth.

Rowan cleared his throat and tightened the arm around her waist. "I'm sorry, Baby. There is so much the three of us have to talk about."

"Like what?" she asked in confusion.

Ben held his hand out to her. He almost growled at the surge of energy that raced through him when she touched him. He bit back a grin when he saw she was also affected.

"How about we sit down?" Ben said, pointing to a seating area with a sofa and a few chairs.

Rowan and Jenna walked to the sofa and sat on it. His brother took her hand to try to calm her. Ben pulled up one of the chairs so he could sit directly in front of her but not touch her. He kept both legs still on the outside of hers.

"We've got a lot to talk about, Pet."

Jenna stared at him. "Okay."

"Let's start with the threat we've heard about against you." Ben glanced at Rowan and then back. "We want you to know we will protect you. That you're safe with us."

Jenna looked back and forth between the two. "I

don't think it's fair to you. You can't put your lives on hold for who knows how long."

"Actually, we can." Ben thought about how much they should tell her right then. At the beginning of their lives together. "Let's talk about the way you feel. Rowan described the attraction you both had for each other from the very beginning. You felt it also?"

She nodded.

"May we experiment? I want you to let me kiss you and see how it feels."

Her eyes widened. "Wait. What?"

Rowan squeezed her hand. "We've got much to tell you, Baby, but I want you to open your mind. Let him kiss you. From the flush on your face, I can tell you're also attracted to him."

"That's crazy. I'm not like that."

Rowan smiled. "Oh, we know. Kiss him first, and then we'll explain more."

Jenna looked at the hand Ben held out. "Come here, Pet."

She reached for his hand and stood. He pulled her in between his legs. He was enchanted when she was about his height standing while he sat. "Don't be afraid of me. I'll never hurt you."

She nodded, but he could still feel the remnants of her fear even when she tried to hide it.

He cupped her face and brought her mouth to his. He inhaled her scent, which aroused him to the point of pain. It was going to be next to impossible to have to wait to strip her and mate with her, marking and making her theirs.

He knew Rowan had the same problem, but he had not taken her. Instead, he had waited for him so they could do it together. Before then, she would have to know what they were and accept her fate as their mate.

Ben kissed her lips softly at first and instantly felt her reaction and arousal build. She gripped his thick wrists in her hands and opened her mouth. She surrendered herself to him at the first touch of his lips.

Ben groaned and pulled her onto his lap, deepening the kiss, letting his tongue overtake her mouth, eating at her until they both moaned in need. He ran his hand up and down her back before he cupped her ass and brought her tighter against his chest.

"Alpha?"

Ben growled at the interruption.

"We have much to discuss," Rowan reminded him.

Ben raised his head to glance at his brother and saw him smiling but he was highly aroused, too. He glanced back down at her and couldn't stop himself from retaking her mouth. He cursed when the phone on his desk started to ring, and he had to pull back.

"Rowan, take her while I answer the phone."

Rowan stood and lifted her from Ben's lap and pulled her onto his own.

Chapter Seven

Ben walked behind his desk and picked up the phone. He listened for a moment and then hung up. His eyes stayed glued to the couple that would become his family. The three of them would live with each other, have children, and grow old together.

He inhaled and tried to cool the raging arousal racing through his veins. When he felt more in control, he walked to the sofa and sat down beside them.

He looked at Rowan and pulled her legs over his lap. "How is she?"

"Confused, which is natural. She doesn't know what to think about both of us, making her feel this overpowering need."

"We have no choice. We must tell her."

Rowan nodded. "I agree. The sooner she knows, the sooner she can come to grips with it."

"It's starting to irritate me when you guys talk about me as if I'm not here," she complained and sat up. She tried to pull her legs from Ben's lap and then growled when he held her tight.

Both men grinned at her.

"We're going to tell you some things that might make you think we're crazy," Rowan told her.

She started to look apprehensive.

"But you will never be in any danger with us. I want you to remember that," Ben said.

Ben cleared his throat, astonished that he was feeling more nervous than he could ever remember. "Both Rowan and I are wolf shifters."

It took her a moment to let it sink in. "You're what?"

"We are wolf shifters. Half of us are human, and the other is wolf."

"You're werewolves?" she screeched.

Both men cringed.

"No," Rowan barked. "Werewolves are in movies. They give us a bad name. Wolf shifters are real."

"I…"

Ben could feel fear grow in her. "Remember, you have nothing to fear from us."

"How do I know that?"

"Because you are our mate."

She sat in shock for the longest time, making them think she hadn't really heard them.

"Did you hear us?"

She nodded. "Yes, I just don't know what to say. Why both of you?"

Ben shrugged. "Our pack has been known to have menage relationships. It's in our genetics. It's like families that have twins or triplets. If someone in your family has had them, you're more likely to have them."

"How do you know I'm your mate?"

Both men laughed.

"It's your scent."

Jenna gasped and then frowned at Rowan. "You're saying I stink?"

"You smell like a dream to us," Ben told her. "But only us. Other shifters will smell our scent and know you're ours, especially after we mate. Humans won't smell anything."

"We mate?"

"Yes, we make love like humans, but the feelings are more powerful. We also stay aroused for each other and will, to some extent, for the rest of our lives."

"You're saying we'll be together forever? How can you know that?"

"Because with wolf shifter mates, that's all it can be. Especially after we take you together, you won't want to be away from us for very long. You won't be able to. It gets painful. For all of us. If you left now, Rowan and I would always have discomfort."

Jenna looked back and forth. "What if you find another mate?"

Ben shook his head. "There is no other mate for us. We get one chance at it."

Rowan gained her attention. "Before you say anything, I must tell you that we would also die an earlier death than normal if we lived without our mate. No pressure, though," he said and grinned.

She snorted. "I don't know what to believe."

"Would it help if we showed you?" Ben asked.

"How?"

"We'll bring our wolves out. If you see us shift, you won't be able to deny it."

"Will they hurt me?"

Ben shook his head. "No, never, Pet. You're the other half of our soul."

She nodded at Rowan. "Okay."

Rowan lifted her off his lap and sat her in the chair. Both men stood and started pulling off their clothes.

Her eyes widened. "Wait, what are you doing?"

"Our wolves can't wear clothes, so if we don't take them off, they'll rip," Ben explained.

VOLUME TWO

Chapter Eight

She stared wide-eyed as the men slowly took their clothing off and showed more and more of their skin. Both were dark-complected and large. Both had black hair, but Rowan had blue eyes, while Ben's were too, but they were a different shade. She had thought they were dark, but the higher their desire rose, the brighter their eyes got.

Her breath stuttered out when they stood in front of her naked. Both men were highly aroused, making their cocks stand up toward their bellies. Like everything else about them, they were large men. She couldn't grasp how she'd be able to fit one, much less two of them, into her body.

Before one second and the other, instead of two men standing in front of her, two huge wolves were there staring at her.

Her first inclination was to scream and run, but when she looked for an escape, one of the wolves whined and nosed her hand, and the other went to stand between her and the door.

It took forever for her to gain enough courage. Jenna raised her hand and lightly touched the wolf's head between his ears. She could see herself shaking, but she made herself do it. She smiled when she realized it was Rowan from the color of his eyes. She sank her fingers into his fur and rubbed along his sides, making him sigh in pleasure.

"You're so soft," she exclaimed.

She giggled when Ben came up on her other side and laid his muzzle in her lap. "You're both so beautiful." She chuckled and shook her head. "I can't believe I'm talking to two wolves and not freaking out."

Ben was very pleased with her reaction. Her strength and courage made her even more appealing to him. His eyes closed when her hand started stroking his head. Just that touch made his need for her rise, and from her scent, the same was happening to her.

He rubbed his nose against the junction to her thighs, where the scent was the strongest. He almost growled when she pressed her legs together to prevent him from his quest to press his snout against her wet heat and take in every bit of pleasure he was giving her. But he also knew it was too soon.

Eventually, he'd be able to touch her any way he wanted in his human side and his wolf side.

The need to mark her grew until he knew he'd never be able to settle his raging need until he sunk his teeth into her neck. He grunted, getting his brother's attention. When Rowan looked at him, he gestured toward the apartment the brothers shared on the top floor of the building.

Rowan nodded and then shifted into his human. "Do you trust us enough to give yourself to us?"

****

Her thoughts scattered for a moment before all she could think about was having them touch her.

"Yes."

"You'll never run from us and always be ours. Can you handle that?" Rowan asked.

Her heart was pounding so hard she felt it against her breastbone. Although her normal way of thinking tried to stay logical, her instincts told her to give herself to them.

"Y … yes."

Rowan smiled, and if she wasn't mistaken, the wolf did, too.

A startled gasp tore from her when Rowan picked her up and started toward the elevator.

"Where are we going?" she asked.

"Up to our apartment. We'll all live there until we deem it safe enough to buy a house."

Her arms tightened around his neck when, as they rose in the elevator, Ben, in wolf form, was licking every bit of exposed skin on her arms and legs. She should have found it disgusting, but it only made her hotter.

Rowan chuckled when he felt his brother press his nose against her core with only the thin fabric of the skirt between them, and inhaled.

She couldn't believe how much it turned her on to have Ben's fur tickle her thighs and feel his warm breath against her sopping cunt.

Rowan kissed the top of her head. "It's okay to feel aroused. You probably wouldn't enjoy it if we weren't your mates."

That made sense and helped calm her feminine instinct to shy away from Ben.

Her eyes roamed around the large room as they stepped out of the elevator. It definitely looked like a bachelor lived there. There was no color besides tan, black, gray, and white.

Rowan chuckled. "Don't worry. We'll give you full range to decorate our home."

They walked down a long hallway. Some of the room's doors were closed, but the few that were open showed her the same masculine décor.

Her breath caught on a huge bed in the middle of the room. Rowan laid her down in the middle and then came to rest by her side. He held his head up with one hand while the other started to skim over her skin, barely touching her cunt where she needed the most attention now.

Her body jerked when she heard the ripping of fabric at the same time her clothes were pulled from her. Now, she lay naked and exposed to both of them.

Rowan's head lowered, and his lips started tenderly taking hers. One of her hands rose to cup the back of his head.

Jenna tried to roll to her side only to find herself pinned to the bed with a heavy and hairy object. She looked down at Ben as he licked around her belly button and torso.

"Is he going to change back?" she asked.

Rowan grinned. "Yes. Our wolves' taste buds are more sensitive than our human ones. He's just savoring you and getting to know your body. Does it bother you?"

Jesus, it should, shouldn't it? She was being made love to by a man and a wolf.

"I know what you're thinking, but it's not the same as having sex with an animal. Baby, we're shifters, but our minds are always in control and think like humans. We have wolf instincts, but they are never in control of our actions. Does that make sense?"

She thought about it for a moment. "Yes. Ben is still a human but looks and feels like a wolf."

"That's right. Now, let's get back to our kiss."

He lowered his head again, and the kiss quickly got hotter and more out of control. She felt his hands slide down and cup her breast. Her nipples were already as hard as rocks, but he continued to torment them, making her squirm. Well, as much as they'd let her move.

She gasped when Ben turned to his human, wrenched her legs apart, and started to devour her cunt. It felt like he was trying to suck up any drop of her cum but also used his fingers, first one and then two, to make more.

His growling told her he was enjoying himself, but it felt like he'd devour her at any moment.

Every thought in her head splintered as both men set out to make her burn hotter and hotter as the minutes passed.

"Oh, God, please," she begged over and over again.

"Brother, you need to get in her," Rowan said. "I'll hold her against my chest."

It didn't take another word. Ben slid up her body, spreading her legs even farther. He bent and kissed her sweetly on her lips as he lined his cock up to her cunt.

Slowly, he started to press into her.

She felt like she'd split apart and was frantically trying to adjust her hips to get comfortable. "Hey, I can't…"

Ben growled. "Rowan, get at her clit. I'm just about in."

"You got it."

She heard the tone of their voices but didn't understand the words. It didn't matter because within seconds of feeling Rowan press on her clit, a gush of cum slid from her, easing his way even more.

Jenna squeaked as he rammed the last few inches into her.

Ben didn't pause but started to thrust into her with deep, fast moves.

"She's ready," Ben said through clenched teeth.

A ball of light burst in her vision, and her body tightened and then convulsed. A scream erupted out of her as wave upon wave of the greatest pleasure rushed through her. It seemed to go on forever, and she was out of breath as he took a few more thrusts and then groaned. She felt spurts of fluid fill her cervix and then realized he hadn't worn a condom.

Rowan smoothed the damp hair from her face. "We'll never wear condoms."

She glanced up at him. "How did you know what I was thinking? Can you read my mind?" She should have been horrified by the thought instead of just concerned.

Rowan chuckled. "Not really. We can sense your emotions easily, and sometimes you're so open we're able to catch your thoughts."

Ben slid from her body, bent, and kissed her lips. "I'll be right back."

Rowan lifted her before coming down beside her. "Do you think you could take me?"

She wrapped her arms around his neck and nodded. "Yes. Please."

He grinned and mounted her. He was as large as his brother, but since Ben had already stretched her out, it was much easier for him to drive into her.

Jenna had been so worn out, she didn't think she'd be able to get aroused again, but she quickly changed her mind as her body tensed and a fresh wave of need built in her.

This time, her orgasm swiftly hit the pinnacle, and then she was thrown over.

When she finally settled, Rowan was finishing his own pleasure. They both lay against each other, sweat bonding them together as they continued to fight to gain back their thoughts and ease their breathing.

She couldn't hold her eyes open, so she stopped fighting and let herself drift to sleep.

Chapter Nine

Ben leaned against the bathroom doorjamb as he watched his brother ram every inch of his cock into their mate. It was the most erotic thing he'd ever seen, and he wanted more than anything to rip the towel from his hips and dive into his mate again. But he knew she'd be too sore for a day, and he needed to let her heal. The last thing he wanted to do was hurt his Jenna.

Rowan tipped them to the side, still inside her cunt, and held her tightly. This was his cue, he stripped off his towel and lay down behind her. One of his hands slid around her waist before he relaxed against her.

"How's she doing?"

Rowan cleared his throat. "Good. She's tired, but that is to be expected."

"Why don't we rest for a bit and then shower?"

"She hasn't eaten either," Rowan told him.

"We'll get that done."

"Are you going to have time for all this?"

Ben nodded. "Yes. I talked to Dillion, and he's going to let the family know about our mate and give us a few days to get to know each other. He knows to get in touch with me if it's really important."

"When will we mark her?" Rowan asked.

"We'll both have to be in her. One in her cunt and the other in her ass."

Rowan exhaled. "I want it to happen in the next few days."

"Me, too. I don't want to leave this place without her marked."

They both rested against Jenna for several minutes, just absorbing the fact that the three were together, and the men would do everything to make sure she stayed happy and protected at all times.

Ben stretched. "Let's get her clean and then feed her."

"You got it. I'll go start the shower, and you can bring her in."

Ben nodded. He cupped the side of her face. "Jenna. Wake up, Pet. We want to wash you."

She shook her head and tried to push his hand away from her, making him smile.

"Oh, no, you don't." He stood and lifted her into his arms. He laughed when she grumbled and tried to hit his shoulder.

Rowan turned around when they walked into the bathroom. "What's going on?"

Ben grinned. "It seems our mate doesn't like to be woken up, and she's trying to push me away."

Rowan laughed. "She'll learn quickly that pushing us away is never an option."

"Oh, I think she's learning that already."

His brother stepped into the shower and reached for Jenna. He stood her on her feet but kept a tight hold on her when she swayed.

Ben pinned her hair up with a hair tie someone had left in the apartment before reaching for a washcloth and soap. He washed every inch of her body, making Rowan turn her so he could get to her front.

When he finished, Rowan lifted her in his arms and stood off to the side, talking softly to her while he washed himself. When he finished, he took her from his brother and stepped onto the rug before reaching for a towel.

"I can stand," she said.

"We want to make sure you're strong enough."

She sighed. "I am. I'll hold onto you."

He studied her face before setting her on her feet. "Hold onto the counter while I dry you."

She did as he asked. When he finished with her, he wrapped another towel around his waist.

"We need to feed you, Pet," Ben told her and lifted her again.

She rolled her eyes. "Are you ever going to let me walk on my own?"

You could hear Rowan chuckle behind them as he carried her into the closet. He set her on top of one of the dressers before reaching for one of his shirts to put on her. His eyes never left her as he secured a few of the buttons. He then caught the pair of shorts his brother tossed him and slipped them on.

"I'll go start something," Rowan said and walked out.

"Are you hungry, Pet?" Ben asked as he lifted her again, ignoring her snort.

"I guess a little."

"You need to keep your strength up, and we won't let you go without a meal."

Her arms snaked around his neck as they walked down the hallway. "Why do I feel so good? I had a headache and a few mild pains, but they're all gone."

"You'll get stronger the more we mate. When you take our cum into your body, it changes your DNA."

"Will I become a shifter?" Jenna asked.

He shook his head. "No, but you will be stronger than the average human, and you'll definitely live longer and age slower."

He set her on one of the stools at the island before taking three glasses from the cupboard and juice from the refrigerator. He placed one in front of her and filled her glass. "Drink. This has a lot of vitamins in it."

She took a sip and then looked at him in surprise.

"This is good. What is it?"

"It has fruits and veggies that keep our bodies strong. Now, you'll drink it," Rowan said as he placed a bowl in front of her.

Ben watched her look down in surprise. Rowan had warmed up the spaghetti that one of the pack members brought them.

"Did you guys make this?" she asked.

"No. A friend did."

She took a bite and then hummed as she chewed. "Oh, wow, this is delicious. Can I get the recipe from him?"

Ben glanced at her as he sat down on one side of her and Rowan on the other. "It was a female pack member."

He felt her stiffen.

"What's wrong?" he asked.

"I know it's probably not my place, but I won't be able to handle being around your women."

Ben tilted her head to face him. "For one thing, we don't have women. I can't say we haven't ever had sex, but you're the only one we could ever love, and since you came into our lives, there will never be another woman. Some of the female pack members bring us meals and clean the place. If that makes you uncomfortable, we can ask them to stop."

"Let me think about it. Okay?"

He nodded and leaned forward to kiss her lips before releasing her to eat his own meal. When they finished, all three cleaned up, which didn't take long.

"Let's go sit on the sofa and talk," Ben suggested, following her into the living room.

They sat on either side of her, and each put their hands on her. One was on her thigh, and the other took her hand.

"I'm sure you probably have some questions," Ben said.

"Yes." She inhaled. "I assume I'll be staying here."

Rowan nodded. "Yes. You'll never be without us. You'll never spend another night alone."

She nodded. "Can I get my things from the apartment?"

"We'll have men go and pack up your things and bring them here," Ben told her.

"They won't know what's mine," she said.

"One of us will go with them…"

"But you won't know either," she murmured.

Ben squeezed her thigh. "Yes, we will. We'll be able to tell by your scent what is yours. If we make a mistake, we'll take it over to where they're holding Nicole."

Jenna nodded, but he could tell she wasn't convinced. He knew with time, she'd know them better than anyone and vice versa. But first, they had to eliminate the threat against her.

VOLUME TWO

Chapter Ten

Jenna leaned back against the sofa.

"What's your next question?" Ben asked.

"You talked about me living longer."

Ben nodded his head. "Yes. Not as long as a shifter but much longer than the average human."

"How long is that? How long is your lifespan?" she asked.

"We can live up to one hundred and fifty years," Rowan said.

"I've known of a few that lived longer than that," Ben said.

Her eyes were wide. "There's no way I'll last that long."

Just the thought of the world without them gave Jenna a strong sense of panic and muted devastation. It was crazy since she'd just met them, but she already felt a bond grow that she never knew could be so strong.

"How old are you?" Rowan asked.

"Twenty-three," she said. "How about you guys?"

"I'm sixty-eight, and Rowan is sixty-five," Ben told her.

They both laughed when her mouth dropped open.

"Oh, wow." They looked so young. She presumed they were older than her, but she would have never guessed they were over forty years older.

"Will you ever age?" She hated the thought of them being young studs while she grows into an old woman.

"Yes," Rowan said. "It will take longer for us to show our age, but it will happen."

Jenna wanted to ask what would happen when

they no longer found her attractive, but she decided to let it go for now.

"Any other questions?" Ben asked her.

"Not at the moment, but I will eventually."

Ben squeezed her thigh. "You can ask us anything at any time. You're our priority now."

That surprised her. "Aren't you the alpha?"

"Yes. Both Rowan and I lead the pack, and there will be times when one of us will have to leave the building, but the other will stay in the area. We can't be away from each other very much because we will all start to ache physically."

She was glad to hear that. The thought of being alone and away from them made a kernel of unease build. She knew that eventually she'd get used to it, but until then, she'd have to stay strong and not complain. That was the last thing her mates would want or need.

"I'll go call some of our guys to pick up your things. Why don't you and Rowan find a movie to watch?"

She nodded and watched him go.

Rowan squeezed her. "He'll be back, Baby."

It was ridiculous to miss him already, especially when he was just in another room. She turned her attention to the TV while Rowan browsed through some channels until they found one they both liked.

Ben came back and sat down on her free side, and laid his hand on her thigh. It seemed both always had their hands on her, and she loved it. She never thought of herself as a touchy-feely kind of person until she met them.

She watched the sunset, making the room dark except for the light from the TV. Two huge, strong men were on either side of her, and she admitted to herself that this was the only time she'd felt truly safe in her life since early in her childhood. When she was a child, she found out that monsters really existed and realized that life was unpredictable and she had to be careful.

Jenna had discovered the hard way when her friend Lacy's mother was kidnapped, raped, and murdered. She knew her friend would never be the same happy-go-lucky person she'd been before the tragic incident.

She'd tried to be there for Lacy, but her family was broken, and her father was doing the best he could to keep it together. They had moved when the girls were twelve, and she hadn't heard anything from her since. She'd often thought of trying to find her, but she was afraid she'd just bring back memories her friend would have to deal with again.

"I know it's early, but I think you need some sleep," Ben told her.

Jenna nodded. "Where will you guys be?"

Rowan chuckled. "With you, Mate. We will rarely be apart."

She smiled and then squeaked when Ben lifted her into his arms. "This is getting ridiculous, Ben."

Rowan laughed as he walked behind them. "Good luck trying to change him."

Jenna grinned when Ben just rolled his eyes.

Ben walked into the bathroom, set her on her feet, and handed her a new toothbrush and paste. It was only when the three stood at the counter that she realized there were three sinks.

Jenna wiped her mouth with a towel Rowan handed to her. "Did you guys plan the bathroom yourselves?"

Ben nodded. "We designed the bathroom with the hope we would find our mate."

Jenna caught the heat of arousal mixed with

satisfaction and joy. She was pleased she made them happy. She had no idea how fate operated, but she was pleased with how it worked out for them.

Rowan lifted the blanket. "Hop in, Sweetheart."

Jenna slid into the middle and was instantly surrounded by male muscle and heat.

She smiled as the men arranged her the way they wanted her. She ended up against Ben's side with her head on his chest and then with Rowan curled around her backside.

There was no way in hell she'd ever be cold if they slept like this every night.

Chapter Eleven

The next day, Jenna was at the kitchen island making a list of things she needed. Ben was in his office a few floors down, and Rowan was in the shower.

She was surprised when the elevator door opened, and two very pretty females walked into the apartment like they owned the place.

"Can I help you," she said as she stood and faced them.

Both stopped in their tracks.

"Who the hell are you?" one of them said.

"How about you answer my question first?" Jenna said, crossing her arms over her chest.

The woman growled and took a step forward when the other one grabbed onto her arm to stop her.

"Morgan, smell her. She's Alpha and Beta's mate."

The one called Morgan lifted her face and sniffed. The color drained from her face, leaving her pale, and then her complexion immediately turned red.

The one that stood beside Morgan stepped forward. "Hi, I'm Noelle, and that's Morgan. It took us by surprise because we hadn't heard anything about you."

Rowan walked into the room and stood by Jenna. "That's because we haven't officially introduced her."

Morgan sneered. "Why? Because she's a human?"

Jenna heard Rowan growl and looked up to see him scowling at the woman. "No, we have a situation we need to deal with. Now, tell me, Morgan, why are you here, and why do you think you can question me?"

Noelle took another step into the room and tried to smile. "I'm sorry, Beta. We were just surprised. Morgan didn't mean anything by it. We are here to clean, and we brought a casserole for you."

"I appreciate that," Rowan said. He looked down at her and smiled. "Would it be okay if they cleaned the apartment this time? It will give you time to decide how you want to deal with it."

Jenna didn't want to be anywhere around the woman, but she wasn't going to rock the boat. "It's fine. I'd appreciate it."

Rowan bent and kissed her lips. "I'll be in the office, three doors down."

"Okay. I'm just making out a few lists," Jenna said.

"You could always do that in the office with me. I have a comfortable sofa."

"I'll come in later," Jenna said.

Rowan turned and walked away. She heard a door close before she turned back to the women. "Is there anything I can help with?"

Morgan's eyes narrowed. "No. Just stay out of our way."

Jenna raised her hands. "Fine by me."

She turned to go back into the kitchen when she heard Morgan.

"By the way, the sofa is very comfortable. I've spent many hours on it."

Jenna looked over her shoulder. "Good for you. It will never happen again."

She walked away, listening to them argue. They were whispering, but she knew Morgan meant for her to still hear.

"I can't believe you're being so mean," Noelle

said.

"I can't believe you're not angry," Morgan said. "You had hoped to be with them, too."

"But we always knew we weren't their mate."

"True, that doesn't mean you couldn't have had a relationship with them. They could have still fucked one of us, and we could have had a relationship, but they would never love us. But seriously, I couldn't care less about that. I just want to be with them for the status I'd get."

"Come on. Let's get this done before the alpha gets back," Noelle said.

Noelle set the pan in the refrigerator. "You just need to bake this at 350 degrees for an hour."

At least one of them was nice. "Thank you."

The two started in the living room and then moved to the kitchen. Jenna didn't want to be in their way, mainly because Morgan kept making comments about fucking the guys, and she couldn't take any more.

Jenna gathered her papers and walked toward Rowan's office.

"They can still fuck us," Morgan murmured, and Jenna knew she wanted her to hear her.

Jenna turned toward her. "No, they can't. They are mated now. They wouldn't be able to touch another woman."

Morgan smirked. "Is that what they told you?"

Jenna pressed her lips together. She didn't want to argue with the woman and didn't care if she never saw her again.

"Think about this. That is true if you were a shifter like us, but you're a human. They don't get the same bond with you as they would us."

****

Jenna walked into Rowan's office and closed the door behind her. She tried to smile when he looked up from his desk. His smile turned down when he got a look at her.

"What happened?" Rowan said as he stood and walked to her.

Damn. She'd always been bad at hiding her emotions.

He took ahold of her shoulders, bent, and looked her in the eyes. "Tell me, and don't you dare lie to me."

"H-have you ever fucked those women?"

Rowan sighed and led her over to the sofa. He set her things down, sat, and pulled her onto his lap. "My brother and I are over sixty years old, so yes, we have had a few of the women. But please believe me when I say now that we have you, there is no way in hell, both emotionally and physically, we could ever fuck another woman. It makes me sick to even think about it."

Jenna still didn't know how she felt about the situation, but she did know she didn't want those women around. "I think I can take over the cleaning and cooking," she said.

"Are you sure? I can get others to help."

"The apartment isn't that big, and since I can't go to work, I could take it on. Let me try it myself first. I'll ask for help if I need it."

Rowan grabbed a chunk of her hair at the back of her head, tilted her head up, and smashed his lips to hers. Just the simple contact was enough to make her body's desire increase to the point she was practically already begging him for more. She heard him growl when she pressed her breasts against his chest.

Rowan twisted around and laid her on her back on the sofa. Morgan's words came back at her.

"Wait."

Rowan lifted his head. "What, Sweetheart?"

"I don't want to make love on the sofa."

He looked perplexed.

"Morgan implied that you guys had fucked on it," she told him.

He got a hard glint in his eyes that would have scared her had she not known he'd never hurt her.

"We have never, and I mean never, taken a woman in this apartment. We were keeping it clean in hopes that we'd find our mate. Now that you're here, your presence will fill every corner, and every shifter will know this is your home and respect it. I will have the alpha talk to Morgan. I won't let her around you. No one will be able to upset you and get away with it."

She exhaled and nodded. That made her feel better. She wrapped her arms around his shoulders. "Kiss me again."

He chuckled. "Of course. It would be my pleasure."

Rowan spent the next hour making love to her with his hands and mouth, and it wasn't until later that she guessed both women would have heard them and maybe even smelled their arousal and cum. She should have been embarrassed, but instead, she was glad they were there. It would show them without words who the mate was.

VOLUME TWO

Chapter Twelve

Two days passed, and Ben was frustrated. He had several of his best men out looking for the bastard, but they had not been able to track Payne down.

He took a long sip of his drink, leaned his head back against his office chair, and closed his eyes.

Ben could hear and smell his mate and brother as they cuddled on the sofa, and he wanted to be a part of it. He was about ready to burst with the need to mate and mark Jenna. He decided tonight was the night it would happen. They'd given her a few days to heal from their first bout of sex, and besides his brother feasting on her cunt, they hadn't touched her in a sexual manner.

Ben finished his drink, stood, and walked out of his home office and into the family room. He stood back and watched the two most important people in his life, and he couldn't have been more pleased. The only shadow was that bastard, Payne, but he knew he'd eventually find him and then put him down like the vile animal he is.

He didn't even glance at the TV as he walked around the sofa, sat on Jenna's side, and slid his hand between her thighs. He could feel that little caress was all it took to get her hot.

Rowan turned his head and watched as he lifted the thigh closest to him. He nodded at him to do the same.

A gasp tore from her mouth when both of her legs were spread wide and held in their tight grip.

Ben used his other hand to caress her inner thighs and cunt. Within a few minutes, she was begging them to take her. He could feel the mating heat soar to a level that matched his own.

"Tonight, we mark you. Do you know what that means?" Ben asked her. He smiled when she didn't answer because all her attention was on what they were doing to her. "Pet, listen. My brother and I will both mate and mark you at the same moment."

"Mark? What does that mean?" she asked.

Ben held her down as she squirmed but continued to play with her cunt. "It means we'll both sink our teeth into your neck, and then no shifter anywhere in the world won't know who you belong to."

"Will it hurt?"

Both men laughed.

"From what I've heard, it's supposed to make you wild, but in a good way," Ben told her.

Her head fell back when he thrust two fingers into her tight cunt, and Rowan had unbelted her robe and started tormenting her tits. They needed her to be as hot as possible to prevent her discomfort when they both took her.

"Let's take this into the bedroom," Ben said. He picked her up and carried her to their bed. He pulled the robe off that they had put her in after the shower. They didn't allow any panties and hid the ones that came from her old place.

Ben stripped off his clothes and lay down beside her. His hand went to her breast, and his thumb slid over her nipple, making it redder than it already was. He glanced at his brother to see him get the things they would need for this ultimate mating and set them up by the pillows.

"You are so fucking beautiful, Mate," Ben said and leaned down and started to kiss her. His hand glided down her body, caressing as much of her as possible. They paused by the crease of her ass to delve in between them and press on her tight ass. "We're going to take this tonight, Mate. We'll both be in you at the same time, making you feel good." He kissed her passionately. "You want that, don't you? You want us to make you so hot you feel like you're burning up inside, but in a good way."

He listened to her murmur her need and cry of pleasure. Then he pressed his fingertip into her ass. He let her get used to it before they went farther. He started to press in, crooning to her as he worked his way all the way in.

Ben studied her expression as his fingers became bolder. He used first one finger, then two and three fingers to stretch out the tight muscle. When she was withering and begging, they knew it was time.

His brother would keep her level of need high fucking her cunt while Ben washed up and came back. He stared at the beautiful woman who was his destined mate and couldn't be happier. He stayed back and waited for his brother to get in her and work her until she was ready for him.

"Ben, she needs you," Rowan said.

"Hold her tight while I work my cock into her. I'm going to go slow so I don't hurt her."

Rowan positioned Jenna against him, with him deep inside her cunt. His hips stopped moving, and he held her against him, holding her for Ben to take her and make her theirs.

Ben's body tensed with the intense surge of desire to see her most private place and to drive as deep as he could into her sweet ass. He wanted to possess her in the most intimate way a man could take a woman. Ben almost orgasmed at the realization he would be the first to take her ass.

He gripped her hip as he worked some lube into

her puckered hole. He gritted his teeth as he started to work his cock into her. He would stop when she tensed, but otherwise, she accepted his invasion, and he was all the way in within a minute.

All three of them moaned at the feeling of being together. It was something that bonded them together when they fucked her like this.

"Let's do this," Ben said, slowly moving in and out of her while his brother did the same. One of them would pull out while the other one pushed in, making a seesaw motion.

He felt her start to tighten and knew she was close. He listened as Rowan whispered encouraging words to her as they sped up.

"That's it, Pet. Take everything we give you."

Jenna was moaning and crying out her need for them to go faster.

"Are you ready?" Ben asked Rowan.

"Yes. Let's do this. Let's make her ours in every possible way," Rowan said and started to pound into her.

"Come for us, Love. Let go."

She shook her head. "No. It's too much," she cried.

Ben bent over her. "You'll do what your mates say, Pet. Come for us, now."

She tightened unbearably. When she let go, both men took a junction of her neck on either side and let their teeth elongate before biting down on her, marking her forever.

Her scream echoed through the room telling them they'd pushed her over again.

She collapsed on Rowan's chest as the men took their own pleasure.

After giving her every drop he had in his balls, he leaned over them but braced his hands on either side of them to prevent him from putting all his weight on them. Drops of sweat from his forehead fell onto her back, and he didn't have the strength to wipe it away.

It took a long time to gain control over his body, and he needed to stand. He'd never had this depth of emotion and pleasure before. Not even close.

He was finally able to disengage from her and stand. He slid his hand over her back and kissed the spot he'd marked.

"I'll be right back, Pet. Relax with Rowan."

After a quick shower, he took the time to clean as much of the sweat, lube, and cum off her. He tossed the cloth into one of the sinks before he made his way back to them. Rowan had managed to get the two of them under the blanket, so Ben just had to slide in and curve his body around hers.

He'd never forget the sounds she made when they fucked her. The mewing, crying out for more, her screams of shock and ecstasy when they pushed her over. They were forever tattooed in his mind, and all he wanted was to make her cry them out again and again.

At the moment, he had to be happy with just holding her, which gave him a different but strong emotion as the sex. He could see them doing this for the rest of their lives.

Chapter Thirteen

Jenna woke up the next morning, started to stretch, and moaned when she felt her muscles cramp and tighten from the loving they'd had the night before. She looked both right and left and saw the men were gone. She didn't understand the disappointment she felt. The men had made her feel things she had never known existed. It had been like an out-of-body experience for her, and it still left her feeling peaceful.

She rolled out of bed and made her way into the bathroom. When she got under the hot spray in the shower, her muscles immediately relaxed. She took her time washing her hair and body. When she was done, she dried off, dressed in the skirt and top she'd worn the day before, and started working on her hair.

A gasp tore from her mouth when the door was jerked open.

Rowan stood watching her with a scowl. "Why are you out of bed?"

Jenna looked at him with her mouth open. "What was I supposed to do?"

"Wait for one of us."

Her mouth snapped shut. "For what purpose? I can get out of bed and bathe myself."

He crossed his massive arms over his chest. "We thought you'd be worn out and need help. We just mated with you last night, and I know it took a lot out of you."

"I'm tired, but I'm not helpless."

If anything, Rowan's expression darkened. "We don't want you to take any chances, so we're going to be protective of you, Sweetheart. I'd ask if you could handle that, but since you don't have a choice, you'll get used to it."

Her eyes widened and then narrowed as she faced him. "Oh, really?"

He smirked, which pissed her off even more.

"Yes." He grabbed onto her so quickly she didn't have time to evade him. He pulled her tightly against his body and wrapped his arms around her. "Jenna, this is new to all of us, so we are going to have to adapt. I can guarantee we'll make you happier than you've ever been, and you'll be our top priority."

That stopped her fight for independence, and she pressed her forehead to his chest. "Yes, I do want that. I also want to make you both happy."

"Just having you in our lives makes us happy. We never thought we'd find you, Sweetheart. Now that we have, we'll do everything in our power to keep you with us."

Jenna nodded. "I understand, but I also don't want to be treated like I'll break easily. In fact, I feel stronger than I ever have."

"That's the mating ritual," Rowan said. "Both Ben and I marked you, and we'll keep doing it. But every time we sink our teeth into your neck, our saliva is put into your bloodstream, which alters your DNA. Every time we come inside of you helps, too."

He turned her to face the mirror and moved her head to the side. "See these marks?"

She leaned forward and then gasped as her fingers flew up to trace the marks on both sides of her neck. They didn't stand out, but in the light she could see them.

"Will they disappear?" she asked as she turned her head back and forth.

"For the most part. Every shifter will be able to see them, and they will also be able to smell us on you. But the average human won't."

Jenna studied them a little more. "Why didn't I feel this?"

"Because we made sure you were at the height of your desire and ready to come so you wouldn't feel it."

Rowan stood behind her with his hands on her shoulders. It felt like he was trying to see inside her head.

Jenna cleared her throat. "What's going to happen today?" she asked.

"The three of us will stay here. We need to get to know one another and spend time together. Ben would have to leave if there was an emergency, but otherwise, he's taken time off."

"Where is he?"

"Kitchen. We made breakfast for you. We were going to bring it to you in bed, but you ruined it."

She bit her lip to keep from smiling at his petulant tone. "I'm sorry."

His eyes narrowed when he studied her expression. She tried to look innocent, but she didn't think she was pulling it off.

He sighed and held out a hand. "Let's go before the food gets cold."

She took his hand and let him lead her into the kitchen, where Ben stood at the stove. Ben looked at her, and one of his brows rose.

"I see she wasn't where we thought she would be," Ben said.

She almost rolled her eyes. "Guys, I didn't know I was supposed to stay in bed. Maybe next time you can leave a note."

Both men looked at her in surprise, but she also caught a mixed level of excitement at her sarcastic tone. The intense look in their eyes should have frightened her, but instead, it made her body hum as desire built.

"If I didn't know you were sore, Pet, you'd be

buck naked and back in bed."

Her mouth snapped shut as she stared at Ben. He was right, she was sore, but it didn't deter her body from turning into a needy woman who was achingly ready for them.

Ben grunted and turned back to the stove. "Breakfast is about ready. Why don't you two set the table and get glasses of juice?"

Rowan showed her where they kept everything as they finished setting the table.

A plate was set in front of her, and the sight made her mouth water. A few puffy pancakes were next to strips of bacon and a small mound of scrambled eggs.

"This looks delicious," she said and took a bite. They ate in silence for a minute. "Oh, wow. These pancakes are wonderful."

"Thank you. Rowan and I had to learn to cook because we didn't want any women in this kitchen."

"Why?" she asked.

"Because we want our mate to be the only woman," Ben told her.

Jenna loved the idea. "No other women have been here?"

Ben shook his head. "The only women we allow in are to clean and leave meals for us. The pack knows what we want, so the women don't try to come here thinking anything will happen."

She loved hearing that, and she also liked knowing Morgan had lied to her. She cleared her throat. "I enjoy cooking, guys, so you won't have to worry about starving or having people bring us meals."

"Good. I know how to cook, but I'm not great at it. Ben is better."

"I'm better at a lot of things," Ben said and grinned.

Rowan rolled his eyes. "Maybe a few, but I'm better at other things."

She smiled as the two started to argue about who was better at what. It was fun to watch because they were enjoying themselves and not really fighting.

The three cleaned up the kitchen.

"When will I get my things?" she asked. "I can't keep wearing these same clothes."

"Who said you had to wear anything?" Rowan said.

"I'm not walking around here naked," she snapped and crossed her arms over her chest. A shiver raced down her back when both men faced her with every bit of male arrogance she expected from them. She just hadn't thought it would turn her on.

"If we wanted you naked, Pet, you would be."

"What if I don't want to be?" she asked.

"We know you're nervous right now," Rowan said. "But when you become more comfortable, we'll insist on you not wearing clothing sometimes."

She almost smirked but kept her face bland. Well, they'll see about that.

Ben wrapped an arm around her waist. "Our men are bringing your things later this morning. They didn't want to be followed, so they went to another apartment building. When they know it's safe, they'll come here. We don't want you in any danger, and it looks like Payne is going to be a problem."

She nodded. The last thing she wanted to do was come face to face with that sociopath.

VOLUME TWO

Chapter Fourteen

Several weeks passed, and they had yet to find Payne. Both men were getting impatient, and she knew she was starting to get anxious at the thought of the man being free and close.

Ben started going to his office every day. She knew he could only take so much time, and the pack needed him. It helped to know he was always in the building.

Rowan had his own work to do but tried to do most of it at the apartment.

Jenna had spent some time every day looking online for pillows and pictures for the apartment. She was sick of the dull tones of the men's decor.

She was looking through one of the decorating magazines the men had bought her when the elevator doors slid open.

She was surprised to see Noelle. The woman was smiling, but there was tension about her, which Jenna didn't understand. She'd only seen the woman a few times when she had dropped off food for them.

"Hi, Noelle. Is there something I can help you with?" Jenna stood to face the woman.

"Hey, Jenna. Where are your mates?"

"Ben is in his office, and Rowan is dealing with something but will be right back."

Jenna's eyes widened when the woman pulled a gun from her pocket.

"What are you doing?" Jenna asked.

"You need to come with me," Noelle said.

Jenna could see her getting more and more agitated the longer they stood there, but she wanted to distract her and give Rowan some time to get back.

"Why are you doing this?"

"Because I'm sick of humans taking our men. I can't stand the thought of being with a human man. They are so pathetic and weak. I don't care if the human is my mate or not."

"We didn't have a choice, Noelle. You know that."

Noelle waved the gun around. "Come here, now. We've got to go before the men get back."

Jenna crossed her arms over her chest. "You know they will kill you when they find out you're threatening me."

"Shut up!" she screamed.

Jenna hoped someone would have heard her and come to see what was happening.

"What if I say no?"

"Then I kill the person that comes out of the elevator."

"You'd kill your Alpha?" Jenna asked.

She could tell the thought upset the woman, but she didn't lower the gun.

"If I must. Now, come on."

"I expected this from someone like Morgan but not you. I was hoping we could be friends," Jenna told her.

The woman sneered. "Not going to happen. I only like being with shifters. I'm getting pissed, cunt. Get over here, or someone's death will be on your conscience."

The thought of one of the men getting hurt sickened her and gave her the courage to walk over to the woman. Jenna cried out when she latched onto her arm, digging her nails into her skin. The woman was much stronger than she was and easily dragged her to the elevator. Once on, she pushed a number to a floor Jenna had not been to.

"Are you going to kill me?"

Noelle snorted. "No. I'll give you to someone who will, though."

Jenna had a sick feeling in the pit of her stomach. She took a guess. "You know Payne?"

Noelle chuckled. "Very well. The man is a sick bastard, but he knows how to fuck."

"I didn't know dogs and cats fucked each other," Jenna said.

That pissed the woman off, and she jerked her closer. "You don't know what the fuck you're talking about, so I'd advise you to shut the fuck up."

"Do you really think my mates won't know it was you that took me from them?"

She caught the fear in the woman's eyes but didn't get a response.

The elevator doors opened. Jenna looked around at the crates and boxes stored in the large room. She also frantically searched for a weapon.

They got to another door. Noelle opened it and shoved her through. "Move."

This room was brighter than the other and contained fewer things. Noelle kept pushing her toward another door, which she knew would take them outside.

Jenna tried to keep her cool. She was relieved to see a box cutter on the table before them. Acting as if she stumbled, she snatched up the knife, holding it tightly to her side.

A set of metal steps led down to the ground. When she saw the big black car, her panic started to rise. The door opened, and Noelle shoved her in. When Jenna finally got seated, she stared into the empty, black eyes of the monster who had been harassing her. The car had two seats that faced each other, and she moved to get as far from him as possible.

"Well, well, if it isn't the cunt I've been looking for," Payne said and grinned. He looked at Noelle. "I didn't believe you could do it, Sweets."

Noelle smiled. "I told you I could. Now, I need to get back before they miss me."

Payne pulled out a gun and pointed it at Noelle. "Not so fast, Dear."

Noelle's eyes widened. "Wait, what are you going to do?"

"I have no more use for you," Payne told her.

"But I got the woman you wanted."

"Yes, and I think you for that, but..." He raised the gun and shot Noelle in the middle of her forehead.

Jenna was beyond shocked, too staggered to scream or react, and couldn't fathom what had just happened. The sight of the man so easily taking another person's life, actually enjoying it, made her sick. The fact she hadn't heard a shot confused her at first until she saw the silencer on the gun Payne held.

The feeling of stickiness covered her face, making her reach up. When she brought her fingers in front of her, they were red with blood and what looked like brain matter.

She looked at the man. "What? How could you be so sick?"

Payne's eyes narrowed on her as he yelled to one of his men. "Drive. Take us to the warehouse on Tenth."

"You got it, Boss."

Jenna ignored Noelles body in the seat next to her and struggled to stay upright as the car turned right and then left. It couldn't go very fast because of the other traffic, which gave her men time to find her. Oh, God, she hoped and prayed they found her before this monster could touch her.

Payne put the gun away and sneered at her. "I smell those bastards on you. It's disgusting."

"They are my mates," she informed him. "They'll stop at nothing to get me back. You fucked with the wrong shifters."

She thought she saw some emotion in the man's eyes instead of the cold, dead look he usually had, but it went away too fast to determine what it was.

"That cunt didn't tell me that," Payne growled. "Oh, well, it's too late now." He grinned. I'll be done with you before they get a chance to find you."

Jenna considered all the different scenarios and knew she would have to act before they reached their destination.

As the minutes ticked by, her fear grew and panic started to take over. She kept telling herself to stay calm, but it was getting next to impossible.

She looked out the side of the window to see what seemed like a hundred people milling about going on about their day while she was fighting for her life.

VOLUME TWO

Chapter Fifteen

Rowan stormed into Ben's office.

"What's going on?" Ben asked.

"She's gone. Someone took our mate."

Ben jerked to his feet. "How do you know?"

"Take a second and feel her."

He closed his eyes and concentrated on his mate. Fury and fear built when he felt the terror she was in. He looked at his brother. "What do you know?"

"The only other person's scent I picked up was Noelle's."

Ben was stunned. "She took her. But why?"

Rowan pushed the button for the top floor. "Yes. I sensed Noelle's anger, and a bit of fear mixed in with our mates."

They rushed into the apartment and hurried through every room. Ben picked up the scent at the elevator. "Let's follow. Call our men and have them canvas the area and be ready for anything."

Rowan was on the phone when Ben stopped the elevator on the floor that was used for storage. They walked through the room, following her scent, and went to the outside door.

Ben's fear grew when he saw the ladder had been put down and felt Jenna's distress grow. But what really got to him was the scent of the man, Payne, they'd been looking for. The thought of her in that monster's hands made him want to shift and howl. It took everything not to stay focused.

"Every man in the vicinity is out looking."

"Good. I want to get a car, but it would be hard to follow her scent that way. With all the people and polluted air, it's going to be difficult enough."

"Let's go. If one of us has to change, we will. People will think it's a person and large dog walking."

They made it a mile when Ben finally made the decision. It was going to slow for him. "Shift and get us to her."

"You got it." Rowan walked behind a stack of boxes and came out a second later in his wolf.

"Good. Let's go," Ben said, following his brother as he rushed through the streets. Several people were startled when they saw Rowan, but Ben ignored them.

Rowan was taking them into the warehouse part of the city. Now, they had the scent of ships to contend with.

"You still got her?" Ben asked.

Rowan nodded and kept running. They were yards from her when something happened to create chaos with the people who took her. Oh, God, please just protect her.

They rushed around a corner to see Jenna with blood all over her, Payne on the ground, and his men fighting and trying to keep her from running.

Ben turned to his wolf, and with his brother, tore into the men that touched their mate. A few were able to shift and run off, but they got the majority.

He shifted back and walked over to Jenna, who was sitting on the ground with a box cutter in her hands and shaking.

"Easy, Mate," he said, taking the knife and throwing it away. He picked her up and got them both in the car. "Call someone to meet us. We need to get away from here before the police arrive."

"I'll drive us," Rowan said. "You just take care of our mate."

"You got it."

Rowan closed their door, and Ben heard the motor

start. They started moving. He held her tightly against his chest and crooned to her until she settled a bit.

"We got you, Pet. It's Ben. You're safe." He said it over and over again until she looked at him and focused.

"Ben?"

"Yes, Mate. I've got you."

Her breath hitched. "I was so scared."

"I know. I'm so sorry. No one should have ever had the chance to take you."

She pressed her hand against his chest. "No. Noelle just came at the right time. It was the only time I'd been alone in the apartment, and both of you were nearby."

"Noelle? What did she do?"

"She had a gun, and she made me go with her."

Ben's brows snapped together. "But why?"

"She hated humans and hated the fact that some of the shifters had human mates. She wanted you to."

"But she wasn't our mate," Ben said. "What did she have to gain?"

"As long as she was with you, she didn't care about you guys loving her. She just wanted you and the status it would bring her. Did you see her body?"

He shook his head. "No."

"A few guys pulled her out of the car and dragged her somewhere as Payne fought to get me out of the car."

"You cut him?"

She nodded. "Yes. His throat. He's dead, right?"

Ben kissed her forehead, ignoring the blood and other fluids. "Yes, Mate. We're so proud of you."

The car stopped, and then the back door opened. Rowan slid in, took her legs, and laid them over his thighs, then the car started moving again.

"How is she?" Rowan asked.

"I think she'll be okay," Ben said. He told him about Noelle and what happened to her. We went on to tell him about the box knife Jenna got and how she slit the monster's throat.

Rowan squeezed her leg. "We are so proud of you, Sweetheart."

Ben still couldn't get the thought of her being taken from them so easily out of his mind. He stared at the two as they talked softly to each other.

Rowan got his attention. "Is all the blood from just Payne?"

He shook his head. "No. He killed Noelle, who sat beside her."

"Jesus Christ," Rowan burst out before cuddling up with Jenna.

They made it home within minutes. Ben hoped no one was around when they brought Jenna out of the car. It might look frightening to see two naked men with blood smeared on them and a woman covered in blood.

He didn't care. He just wanted to get his mate taken care of.

Chapter Sixteen

Jenna kept her arms around Rowan's neck when he carried her as the three rode the elevator up to their place.

The three went right into the bathroom, where they stripped her of her bloody clothes. The three stepped into the massive shower, and then the men took a long time to wash every part of her.

She had been shaking before, but it got worse until she couldn't hold herself up without help. It was easy because the men's hands hadn't left her body since they found her.

"Easy, Pet. We've got you," Ben said with his arms around her holding her steady for Rowan to wash her backside.

"How did you guys find me so quickly?" she asked.

"Rowan picked up your fear right away when he walked into the apartment. We immediately started to follow your scent around the city until we got to you."

"I remember after I c-cut Payne, his men went crazy. It was like they didn't know what to do, but then I saw you guys, and I remember collapsing to the ground because my legs couldn't hold me any longer. I knew you'd take care of me."

Ben pressed his lips to the back of her head. "Oh, Pet, there is nothing we wouldn't have done to get you back. I think I can speak for my brother when I say we're both horrified that he was able to get his hands on you and get one of the pack to help him."

"Noelle told me they had fucked several times, so she's known him for a while. I can't believe he just shot her like it was nothing. How can anyone think like that?"

They dried her off with a towel and set her on the counter to take care of her hair. It felt good having their hands on her again.

"We'll never know, Sweetheart," Rowan said. "I think some people are so tortured that they become one, but I know some are born that way, and Payne was one of those. He enjoyed hurting people. Nothing was going to change him."

Ben looked at Rowan. "That reminds me. We need to call our guy in the police department and tell him about Payne's death."

"Oh, God, do they have to know I was the one that killed him?" Just the thought of going to jail made her stomach churn.

Ben shook his head. "No. We'll just inform them he's dead and where to find the body. Our contact will make sure they don't put a lot of work into finding out who did it. They'll just be glad the man is dead."

Rowan finished drying her hair before he picked her up. "I don't know about you guys, but I need some time to just be with you."

She nodded. "Me, too."

The three fell into bed and wrapped themselves around her. They held her so tightly that it would have smothered her under regular circumstances, but they all needed the closeness more than ever.

Jenna found herself needing them even though she was exhausted. She knew she would never be able to sleep as wound up as she was.

"Guys, I need you to fuck me."

She was facing Rowan, saw the light in his eyes brighten, and heard Ben moan behind her.

Ben jerked her to lie on her back between them. "We need it too, Pet, but I have to warn you that the way we feel, the fear and hostility still filling us, it's going to be hard to hold back."

"We need you so much that we'll take you fast and hard, but you have to promise you'll tell us if you are in any pain," Rowan said.

She shook her head. "I don't care. I need you both inside of me now, or I feel like I'll break into pieces."

Without another word, Ben pulled her onto his chest and started kissing her with a desperation that matched her own. She was already wild and begging from just the kiss.

Rowan sat behind them and started to finger-fuck her cunt to get her ready to take Ben.

"Fuck, she's already swollen and sopping wet."

"Good," Ben growled and lifted her a bit. "Line my cock up to her cunt."

Rowan did what he asked and then sat back and waited for his brother to penetrate her.

She knew why he waited, but she needed him immediately, too.

"Rowan…"

"I know. Give us a second," Rowan said.

She screamed when Ben yanked her down at the same time he lifted his hips, impaling her on his cock and driving it as deep as he could. It was the most wonderful feeling.

Ben thrust a few times and then stopped.

"Wait. Don't stop…"

"Do you want Rowan in your ass, Pet?"

"God, yes," she cried.

Ben smiled. "Then hold still for a second while he gets his cock into you."

Jenna's nails bit into Ben's shoulders as she waited for Rowan to get her ready for him. "Please."

Rowan was gone and back before she knew it, and

then she felt the wonderful pressure as Rowan worked his cock into her tight ass.

She didn't think about it but forcefully pushed herself back, taking his cock in one swift thrust.

Both men yelled.

"You could hurt yourself doing that, Sweetheart," Rowan said as he held her steady and still.

How did she explain the need for them to take her roughly? "I need you guys to give me some pain. I feel like I'll fall apart if I don't get it. I don't know why, and I promise not to break."

"You better tell us if we are hurting you past what you desire, Pet."

"I will."

Jenna felt both men brace themselves, and then they went at her. It was clumsy at first because they needed the violence as much as she did. It finally settled into a pattern. One could thrust hard and as fast as they could.

It was exactly what she needed, and she was basking in the feeling of her men taking her over. They made her feel every inch of their cocks as they slammed into her. They got so deep they penetrated her cervix, which only added pleasure.

"Pet, I need you to come for us. I can't hold off anymore," Ben growled.

"I can't either," Rowan said behind her.

Her body had been tightening up and pushing her toward the orgasm she wanted so badly. Bright spots of light filled her vision before something inside burst, throwing her over. Her scream filled the bedroom.

They continued to pound into her, and then, as she was coming down, she felt their teeth pierce the area between her neck and shoulder. The second orgasm was bigger than the last, and she felt like she would pass out at any moment. Her screams bounced off the walls of the bedroom and were suddenly mixed with their growls and moans.

She tried to hold on so she could experience every bit of pleasure the men were giving her, but she couldn't fight the way her body needed to settle.

The last thing she heard was both men telling her how much they loved her. She tried to say it back, but the curtain of slumber descended on her.

VOLUME TWO

Chapter Seventeen

A few weeks later, Jenna lay on the bed, hugging a pillow to her stomach. The last few weeks had been blissful but also frustrating. She loved these guys more than anything in her life, and she couldn't imagine being without them. But the fact they hadn't let her out of their sight for even a minute was slowly driving her nuts.

She sighed and rolled her eyes when she felt one of them enter the room to check on her.

The side of the bed dipped as Rowan sat beside her. His hand started roaming over her naked backside, pushing the covers off her.

"Hey!"

Rowan chuckled.

She turned her head and narrowed her eyes at him. "Can't you let me sleep?"

Rowan rolled his eyes. "I would if you had been sleeping."

"My eyes were closed, Buster," she grumbled.

He chuckled. "Yes, I saw that, but I can hear your heartbeat, and it was elevated. Baby, you can't hide anything from us."

She snorted. "Oh, I know that. I can't even pee by myself anymore."

"Oh, poor baby. Is it rough having us around all the time?"

"Yes," she snapped.

She knew she was in trouble when Rowan's smile grew. A second later, a large hairy body came over her back and squished her to the mattress.

"Hey!" she cried.

"Well, I guess he heard you, and you're in trouble

now," Rowan said and grinned.

Jenna wiggled her ass. "Get off me, Ben."

The wolf licked the back of her neck and sniffed around her upper back, causing shivers to race down her spine. She stiffened when Ben moved down, pushing her legs apart with his nose. She tried to shove him off, but it was impossible.

"Dammit, Ben. You're being a pervert."

The room got suddenly quiet.

"Oh, shit, now you've done it," Rowan said.

She felt Ben's nose between her ass cheeks and then a long, wet tongue. She couldn't help the arousal that started to build. Ben ate at her for several minutes, but she couldn't lie still anymore and started pushing her hips up and pressing against Ben's tongue.

"Ben…"

"I don't think he's ready to stop, Sweetheart."

Jenna looked to Rowan, who was sitting in a chair, watching them with his fingers interlaced on his stomach and his legs straight out in front of him. It was the large hard-on that grabbed her attention the most. She felt saliva pool in her mouth.

Rowan grinned. "Do you want some of my cum, Love?"

"Yes."

Rowan stood and stripped before coming to the bed. He lay across it and close enough for her to reach his cock. One of her hands grasped it, and then she leaned in and sucked it into her mouth. She would have smiled at the hiss that came out of his mouth if she could.

Jenna kept getting distracted by what Ben was doing to her but tried her best to concentrate on Rowan.

She was startled to feel the fur was gone and then a hot male body behind her. He grasped her hips.

"Hold on tight, Pet."

Without warning, he speared his cock into her asshole until he couldn't go any farther. He didn't wait but went at her like a piston.

"Keep sucking," Rowan growled.

God, it was next to impossible to concentrate as Ben rammed into her over and over. If she hadn't been so aroused, it might have hurt.

"This is one of my favorite places in the whole world," Ben said. "I want you to come for me."

Oh, God, her thoughts were so scattered that she didn't know what to do. She felt Ben reach around her and start tormenting her clit.

That's all it took for her to go over. A scream tore out of her but was garbled because she still had Rowan in her mouth. She felt a gush of fluid fill her as Ben groaned above her.

Jenna had stopped to catch her breath.

"Suck," Rowan demanded.

She started to take him farther into her mouth as Ben pulled out behind her. She felt him kiss her shoulder.

"I'll be back."

She thought she nodded but wasn't sure.

Rowan pulled out of her mouth.

"Hey, wait," she said.

He rolled off the mattress in front of her, and then she felt him pull the pillow from under her where Ben had put it. He then pushed her to lay flat on her stomach.

She tried to open her legs, but Rowan kept them between his. Keeping them tightly together. She was startled to feel fingers separate her ass cheeks, and then the head of Rowan's cock started to penetrate.

Oh, God. "Wait…"

"No," he said. "I'm going to ride you hard and make you as tight as possible."

"It stings, Rowan. Let me part my legs."

He chuckled. "No. I want you to feel like you're close to tearing."

"You want me in pain?"

"No. Never. I'm giving you erotic pain that will take you over."

"I don't know…" Her breath caught in her throat as he worked his way into her. A few times, she almost told him to stop, but then a feeling of euphoria took over.

He didn't stop but continued to fill her with every inch of his cock. When he was in, he didn't give her time to adapt but started to piston in and out of her at a frantic rate. Her body tightened little by little, and she fisted the sheet beneath her, hoping it would make her feel like she wasn't flying apart.

A warm hand pressed between her shoulder blades. "I could watch my brother fuck you all day," Ben said and pressed a kiss to one of her shoulders. "Fuck, that looks tight."

Rowan growled. "It is. It's the most intense feeling I've had. On one hand, it feels like the skin of my cock is tearing away because the grip she has on me is extremely tight, I can barely move."

Ben chuckled. "It looks like you're moving okay from here."

"Just wait until you get in her like this," Rowan said.

"Ben," she whispered.

He lay beside her and rubbed her upper back. "What is it, Love?"

"Hold my hand. It feels like I'm going to explode."

"I need her to come, Ben. Help throw her over."

"It would be my pleasure." Ben worked his hand under her so he could reach her clit.

It didn't take more than two pinches before her

body felt like it would fly apart. She vaguely heard Rowan cursing as he fought to keep fucking her through her orgasm.

Ben's hand tightened on hers. "That's my girl. Let yourself go. Fuck. Seeing you come like this is the most beautiful thing in the world. Can you hear Rowan, Pet? You're strangling his cock."

Jenna knew what he was saying, but there was nothing she could have done about it now because her whole being was fixated on the rolls of pleasure that still ran through her.

When she finally came down, she lay boneless and half asleep. She felt the gush of Rowan's cum in her and then nothing as he pulled out.

Ben continued to caress her back and murmur words of love to her, helping her through this vulnerable time she had after a hard orgasm.

"That's it—just rest. Let Rowan clean you up a bit, and then after we rest, we'll get in the tub together. It will help with any soreness you might have," Ben said against her ear.

She hummed but otherwise stayed quiet.

The mattress dipped, and then she felt Rowan cuddle up to her. Both men kissed and praised her as she floated between sleep and wakefulness.

She heard their breathing deepen and knew they were falling asleep. "I love you guys so much it scares me."

Both men set about soothing her when they saw the tears sliding down her face.

"I love you more than I ever thought possible," Rowan said.

"I would give up everything if I needed to keep this family together. I love you, Pet. We'll never be apart as long as we live."

Jenna hummed and smiled. She loved hearing that. It always made her feel perfect and special.

"I love that, Ben. But maybe you guys could let me pee by myself now?" she asked and grinned.

"We'll see," Ben said as Rowan laughed.

It didn't really matter to her, but she liked to keep them on their toes.

The End

Monsters of New York

Rose Wulf

Copyright © 2025

Chapter One

"E-Excuse me, Mr. Darkhan … you're smoking."

Zeno pulled his unfocused gaze up from the mostly melted ice cubes at the bottom of his glass and forced his grip to loosen before the fragile crystal shattered. It wouldn't do to break the damn thing.

Across from him stood a female he vaguely recognized, dressed in The Gin Room's staff uniform, and shifting her weight anxiously. It took him another moment to process her words, as well as the thin haze of still-rising smoke between them.

Damn. Zeno willed his temper away from the edge before pushing out a smokeless breath. He set the glass onto the table next to the chair he'd claimed earlier that evening and said, "I apologize. It seems I should take myself elsewhere." The Gin Room might have been New York's most shifter-friendly drinking establishment, but they did have rules. Chief among them involved not letting surly dragons lose their tempers. *Well...* He'd tried to slip himself onto the lineup for that night's roster, but it turned out the lineup was booked. For at least two whole goddamn weeks. So, no fight club.

Too many alpha shifters and not enough safe space to let out their aggressions.

"Oh, no, sir, I didn't mean—"

Zeno held up a hand to silence the panicking female. "You couldn't have kicked me out if you'd tried." She let out a low hiss of displeasure at his words as he lifted his wallet and extracted two bills, setting them beside the cracked glass. "One for your trouble, one to replace the crystal." With a final nod, he stepped around her and made his way to the door.

He was still tempted to detour downstairs, but watching the evening's brawl would only make the itch under his flesh worse. Finding somewhere to safely stretch his wings might also have been a good alternative, but he had things to get done. Things that demanded he stay in the city for the time being. Little, irritating, playing-human things. That was the downside to always making sure he had an income stream.

Zeno tilted his head back as he stepped outside and narrowed his eyes up to the sky. It was late, and New York City was not known for its fresh, clean air. But with his vision he could see enough. Even with the city's built-up skyline, there was plenty of space for a dragon to fly. If only he could do so without risking another age of dragon hunts.

There was a reason his kind of shifters were so scattered.

He ground his teeth and continued forward. Nearly four hundred years of searching, and still he hadn't found his fabled mate. He feared sometimes that the century he'd blown off being young and foolish had cost him his future. It made no sense why any dragon wouldn't be scouring the earth for their destined partner. Nearly all shifters were driven by the need to find and possess their mate. Yet still, his continued to elude him.

Spotting his frustratingly grounded transportation, Zeno moved up to the curb and the sleek black car as two young human females rounded the corner ahead. The stench of mixed alcohol wafted around them, thickening with their overly vociferous laughter. Zeno would have been content pretending not to notice them, if not for the way they stumbled to a stop and shouted toward him.

"Hey, Sexy Daddy!" Her words were too loud and slurred badly enough that he had to consciously decipher them. Which made it worse.

Zeno let the fire build up his throat just to feel the burn of it, then pushed it back down. He turned only partially, kept one hand on the door and narrowed his eyes at the pair. One wore full-length pants that might have been painted on and likely didn't cover the crack of her ass—certainly didn't hide the strap of her thong. The other wore a glittery miniskirt and outrageous heels. Both wore tops designed to emphasize their breasts. No one else had joined them while his back had been turned, and somehow, their glaring vulnerability only agitated Zeno more. "I am not your daddy," he said sharply. "And you wouldn't like me if I were."

The girls broke into giggling fits, leaning into each other to stay upright. The brunette turned her head as if to whisper to her friend, but he didn't need his heightened hearing to hear every word. "What a *fox*!"

Zeno rolled his jaw.

The other girl, who was apparently the one who'd first called to him, grinned wider. "A silver fox!"

Zeno turned his back and pulled the door the rest of the way open. He wasn't going to babysit these irksome children.

"He needs a little more silver for that, I think," the brunette said, her slurred words carrying in his wake as he ducked into the car. "Hey! Wait!"

"Daddy fox!"

Zeno slammed the door shut, and for good measure, pressed the lock button. "Drive." Maybe he'd clean up his business situation and put New York behind him for good this time. Maybe the pull he'd felt for this city for the past several decades that had compelled him to keep coming back had been some kind of universal misdirection, a siren song dragging him off course. He leaned back in his seat as the vehicle eased into traffic. That was a thought.

"Home, Mr. Darkhan?" the beta in his driver's seat asked quietly.

"Yes." *For now.*

****

Harmony bit her lips as frustration mounted inside her. How was a person supposed to get a job when so-called entry-level positions required multiple years' worth of relevant experience? *Do they not understand what they're asking?* She jerked the mouse to the side, clicking out of yet another briefly promising option and returning to the list. The imperfect, depressingly small list.

She almost didn't hear her mother's shuffling approach in time to close out of the site and pull up the news article she'd left open in another tab.

"Harmony, that's enough screen time for now."

Harmony dropped her gaze to the digital clock in the corner and barely kept her expression calm. It was a miracle she'd ever managed to graduate, regardless of how many years the process had taken. "I was in the middle of reading something, can't I—"

Linda clicked her tongue, rounded the desk, and reached over Harmony's shoulder. As her finger descended on the button that would shut off the monitor, she said, "You know the rule, Harmony. I gave you an extra thirty minutes since I was busy, but we can't have you poisoning your mind with all the nonsense on the Internet." She pulled firmly on the wheeled chair, dragging until Harmony was awkwardly stretched away from the desk entirely, and spun her to the side. "Now stand up, stretch, and get some lemonade. Oh, and go freshen up. We have company coming."

Anxiety twisted in Harmony's stomach as she stood and stepped away from the desk obligingly. She brushed a wayward strand of dusty blonde out of her face and frowned at her mother. "Company?" *She* certainly didn't have the kind of friends who would just drop by. As far as she knew, neither did her parents.

Linda made a shooing motion at her. "Don't dawdle, sweetheart. Splash some water on your face so you don't look like you've been staring at a screen all afternoon."

The agitation returned in a huff and Harmony twisted away to stomp from the room. *All afternoon? Has she lost it?* Ninety minutes hardly counted as an entire afternoon. She was never going to find a job if she couldn't get some real time on the freaking computer.

"Harmony!" her father shouted from the direction of the kitchen. "Don't stomp! It's unladylike."

She let herself roll her eyes since neither of her parents could see her. Why did she care if stomping was unattractive in a woman? Everything she did was unattractive, apparently, up to and including the way she brushed her hair and the way she ate. She was pretty sure her mother meant the fact that she ate in the presence of others at all, but that wasn't what she'd said.

Her parents controlled every aspect of her life to an unreasonable degree. As a child, Harmony hadn't realized it was strange. She'd been homeschooled in her early years, until the economy and some poor financial choices had forced her mother to get a more traditional job. The strictness had increased when she'd started attending public schools. As the world opened up—the rapid spread of cell phones, and of course the surge of social media—Harmony found herself more locked down.

Sure, she had a cell phone, currently locked in a drawer in her mother's desk, because she was only allowed to have it when she was home alone or when she needed to leave the house without them. But it was limited. They'd even found a way to restrict text messages. She had no online presence at all. It hadn't been until one of her on-campus college days—in itself a veritable crime she continued to await punishment for with nervous anticipation—when she'd finally learned what Facebook looked like. She still didn't understand the concept too well.

She was a twenty-four-year-old woman in the modern age on paper only. She'd failed to escape when she'd turned eighteen, because at the time she had thought merely leaving the house and their shitty neighborhood was enough. She'd made the mistake of thinking her parents would let her be free. That hadn't even lasted a year.

Harmony frowned at the pretty dress laid out on her bed. *Freshen up, huh?* This was more than splashing a little water on her face. There wasn't anything wrong with her comfortable jeans and the respectable, plain shirt she'd put on that morning. After all, the most choice she had on her wardrobe was which day to wear which piece of clothing she hadn't purchased for herself. That was usually the case anyway. Apparently, their expected guest was someone her mother wanted to impress, because this was not a casual around-the-house dress.

For a moment, Harmony was tempted to ignore it. But she knew how that would go, and she was taking enough of a risk just searching for a job behind their backs. She would inevitably catch hell when it all came out, but if she was lucky, she'd have some cash tucked away by then. In the meantime, she needed to not pick unnecessary fights. So she stripped out of her casual and arguably boring clothes, found a bra that would look a little less conspicuous with the dress strappings, and set to work squeezing herself into everything.

She was still standing in front of her bathroom mirror, smoothing out wrinkles and double-checking that she'd attached the right straps to the right hooks, when her mother hollered down the hall. Their guest had arrived. Her stomach rolled.

The dress was uncharacteristically alluring for something her parents might choose. It wasn't scandalous, per se, but it wasn't neck-to-ankles modest either. She liked it, objectively, but she was quickly becoming concerned over what it meant. Loose, breezy short sleeves disguised her thicker upper arms. Lace between straps teased actual bare skin over her sides, so much so that she'd had to change panties, too. The collar was low and flirty, enough to show just a bit of the swell of her breasts and the top of her cleavage. And while the skirt itself hung past her knees, most of the dress was tight. Fitted. Her boobs were practically pushed out and somehow her belly looked flatter than usual, while her hips seemed wider.

Honestly, the more she looked at her reflection, the more she questioned whether her parents had actually laid it out for her. It might have been easier to believe someone had snuck in and left it as a trap.

"Harmony Lace, what is taking you so long?" her mother demanded, barging into the bathroom without knocking. She came up short and her eyes blew wide as she raked her gaze over Harmony's figure.

Harmony turned from the mirror and gestured to herself. "Did you really put this out for me? It's ... not like you." Her mother had never even encouraged her to wear something that qualified as sexy, let alone prompted it.

Linda drew a visible breath and nodded once. Her signature of approval.

Oh, crud. She did. Why did that make it scarier?

"It's a special occasion," Linda said, quieter. Something in her eyes was almost wistful. "I'm glad it fits. I was worried."

Harmony folded her arms across her chest. "I'm sorry my weight disappoints you."

Her mother gave a shake of her head and turned from the room. "Let's go. We're making him wait."

The breath rushed from Harmony's lungs. "Him?" *What the hell is going on?*

"Now, Harmony," her mother said, putting the warning snap in her tone that always got a response.

Harmony jolted into motion even as her nerves amped up. Her mother had dressed her up to meet a special guest, who was a male she also refused to identify. That did not bode well at all. She wanted to spin on her heel and run the other way, but the other way would only trap her. If she wanted out, she had to continue forward. One way or another.

"So sorry to keep you waiting!" Linda called as they neared the end of the hall. Her voice had switched flawlessly to the fake warm, overly saccharine tone she used when she was sucking up.

Harmony's nerves intensified and she swallowed hard. There weren't a lot of people her mother sucked up to. Her feet slowed, but she was still close enough to hear the voice she didn't want to hear.

Patrick Eades, who preferred to go by Ricky, said smoothly, "It'll be more than worth it, if you brought what you've promised."

Chills broke out over her skin and the room spun even as Harmony found herself standing at the edge of the sitting space, the hall suddenly behind her. *What did he just say?*

Ricky's permanently leering brown eyes locked on her and his lips lifted in an expression that made her want to hurl. "Well. Not only did you follow through, but it seems you've even wrapped her up for me." He held out a hand. "Come closer, Harmony. Let me drink you in."

Finally, her feet had stopped moving, locking her in place. Harmony felt as though she could barely breathe. "Wh-what...?"

Her father sidestepped up to her and pressed the tips of his faintly shaking fingers to her back. "Come on, now, Harmony. Let's not keep Mr. Eades waiting."

She was unprepared for the strength behind his touch when he proceeded to push and she stumbled forward.

Ricky snatched her nearest arm as soon as it was within reach, hauling her upright and leaning in until he was close enough that she was forced to smell him. She always had found it ironic that he stank as badly as he did, when he was supposed to be the one with the sensitive nose. "You look fucking *delicious*, Harmony." He licked his lips. "I've been waiting a long time for you."

Was it possible for an entire body to cringe? Because hers did. She recoiled as much as his grip would allow. "Let go of me."

"Harmony," her mother admonished. "You're going with Mr. Eades and you're going to do everything he asks of you, do you understand?"

Horror washed over her and she craned her neck to gape at her mother. Until Ricky crooked a finger around her chin and guided her focus back to him. He'd moved closer to her, so close their bodies were almost touching. He was only an inch taller than her five-foot-five, so it wasn't hard for him to hold her stare in a physical sense. He certainly didn't have to tilt her head back or hold her at a weird angle. If it weren't for the strength in his stocky body, he wouldn't have been that imposing at all.

"You're going to come with me, Harmony Lace," he said, speaking in a low tone. He adjusted his grip on her arm to run his thumb along her wrist. "I've got a space all ready for us." His gaze dropped from hers, his head tilting to the side as he eyed her body again. "Today, I finally claim your tight little virgin cunt."

Harmony held her breath, doing her level best not to say anything stupid. She knew what he was. He wasn't just a pig. He was a monster, through and through. He was stronger than her, faster than her, and with his hands on her, there was not a damn thing she could do to fight him off. She knew that.

Everyone who lived in their neighborhood did. Ricky ran with the monster gang that treated the rest of them like poor, backwater peasants paying some sort of convoluted protection tax. Except the protection they were paying for was protection from the very shape-shifting monsters who were threatening them. And Ricky was one of the worst.

She knew, but she did not understand why, even after the terrible thing he'd just said, her parents remained silent. Compliant. Not until she remembered what they'd said moments earlier and reality slammed into her.

The breath she'd been holding finally rushed out on a long, hard gasp as a single, traitorous tear rolled down her cheek. *They sold me off.*

Ricky's smirk broadened and he leaned closer. His tongue pressed against her cheek, dragging up, tracing the line of her tear as he rumbled with a perverse chuckle.

Her stomach rolled and her heart clenched as ice settled in her veins. Still, her parents remained as statues. The same parents that had treated her like a doll to be sheltered and kept from all forms of contact up to this point. It was too much.

Filled with a sudden surge of fury and devastating heartbreak, Harmony ripped her arm from Ricky's loosened grasp and shoved him away from her with all her might. She let out the loudest shriek of pain and rage she was capable of, needing to release the feelings churning in her chest, and when he stumbled back, she didn't hesitate. She didn't stop to consider the dress she was wearing or the flimsy house slippers adorning her feet. She didn't stop to retrieve her phone. She just ran, making a beeline straight for the front door that hadn't even been properly closed.

"Harmony, wait!"

"Harmony Lace, get back here!"

Even if she'd been tempted to look back, Ricky's roar of outrage would have convinced her otherwise. She didn't understand what had happened, not fully, but she knew one thing for certain.

She couldn't let the monster catch her.

VOLUME TWO

Chapter Two

Harmony didn't know where to go. She knew a couple of people—former classmates—who were still local, but she was hesitant to run to them. Anywhere she went she put people at risk. If Ricky was genuinely pursuing her, where could she really hide? He wasn't human. He could just follow her scent wherever she went. And he wasn't humane enough to mind boundaries. Let alone the value of life.

Ricky had made a point of making sure the neighborhood knew what his claws could do. Harmony had watched once in open-mouthed horror as he'd ripped another man open with one hand. The image had scarred her, haunted her, but as she pushed herself to keep moving in some blind semblance of "forward" now, that memory was all she could really see.

That would be her if she stopped moving. Because her parents had handed her over on a silver platter.

Tears blurred her vision again and Harmony stumbled into the wall of whatever building was closest. She caught herself before she could fully lose her balance, sucking in a ragged breath and forcing the tears down.

How could they? It was hard to wrap her mind around. Nearly impossible. She didn't understand at all.

Harmony pushed off the wall, thinking to aim herself at the intersection just ahead, and she didn't realize the side door to the building that had caught her was opening until an obscenely tall man stepped through. In two strides he was blocking her path and had drawn her full attention, her mind finally focused on something other than her mad dash.

The man was at least a full foot taller than her, putting him at no less than six-foot-five. But his height wasn't the only thing large and intimidating about him. His shoulders were broader than she might ever have seen, and his entire body looked strong, even beneath the obviously expensive button-up shirt and pressed slacks. His biceps stretched the shirt's material just with his arms hanging loose at his sides. The man's hair was a thick, luxurious-looking mane of silver-streaked black that was swept off his face and tied at the base of his neck. The light and dark blend in his hair gave him a distinguished flare to the hard-edged strength he presented. Even the still-dark trim of beard, kept short and barely creeping up over the curve of his jaw, presented like an underscore to his masculine strength.

The man's skin was too dark to be any sort of tan, and too bronze to qualify as black. It made him look exotic. A sense that was enhanced by the entrancing beauty of his dark amber eyes, which struck her as reminiscent of the color of fresh honey. Even as he narrowed those eyes at her while his nostrils flared, likely in irritation that they'd nearly collided, she was captivated. Not even the angry scar that slashed diagonally across his right cheek seemed enough to mar him.

Harmony gave herself a hard shake and took a single step backward. *What the hell is wrong with me?* Sure, the man was gorgeous. He looked like he was probably twice her age and she still felt no shame acknowledging she'd never seen a hotter guy, even on television. That did not mean she could afford to stop and gawk. She cleared her throat, blaming her heightened emotional state for the sudden rush of self-awareness and her inability to hold his burning stare. "I-I'm sorry. I didn't mean to—"

"Why are you in distress?" His voice was rough, almost like he struggled to drag up the question, yet he didn't move a single muscle when he spoke.

She lifted her head without thought, blinking at him in confused surprise. Was she being that obvious? *Is it because of this dress?* She had felt horrendously out of place in it, but what choice had she had? It wasn't like she had a stash of clothes somewhere she could change into. Harmony licked her lips in search of enough breath to answer and another humiliating realization rushed through her. She was probably blushing like an idiot.

Her skin was naturally pale. Every flush showed like a glowing neon sign.

The imposingly alluring man's brow pinched tighter. "Is there somewhere you urgently need to be, or are you fleeing from something?" His amber eyes raked over her and she swore her entire body heated despite that he didn't linger anywhere indecent. "Those are not outdoor shoes, Little Dove."

Everything he said perplexed her more. She didn't know what to answer first, or even if she should try. "I—" *Little Dove?* Was that some sort of endearment, or an insult? "Harmony," she said.

He arched a brow. "Harmony?"

Something inside her clenched at the sound of her name on his lips, in that rough timbre he spoke with. She wouldn't have minded hearing it again, but she needed to get herself in order. This was not a man who gave a darn about her. She still wasn't safe. Harmony drew herself up as best she could, despite the confusing flush and butterfly feeling in her belly, and forced herself to look directly into his eyes. "From," she said. "The answer to your question is 'from.'" She swallowed again. "And I really can't linger. I'm very sorry I almost ran into you."

The furrow in his brow disappeared and one edge of his lips kicked up in a faint smirk that practically made his eyes glow. "I'm not."

Harmony shifted her weight, unable to stand still yet unable to look away. Unable to get moving. *It's too soon to stop moving.*

The stranger took a step closer as a sleek black luxury sedan rolled up to the curb behind him. "I'll have you tell me everything, Little Dove."

Her mouth fell open. "What?"

The next thing she knew, the stranger had an arm around her waist and had hauled her straight up and off her feet. He didn't throw her over his shoulder or swing her into some unnecessary princess carry, but instead lifted her high enough that she could see over his shoulder while he held her chest-to-chest. Then he turned and started walking, his other hand sliding into her hair almost before her senses returned enough for her to try and rear back.

"Just a moment," he murmured into her ear. The lowered vibrato of his voice did things to her traitorous body she couldn't put words to and certainly didn't have time for.

Harmony pushed at his chest, feeling as weak as a newborn in his grasp. "What are you doing? Put me down!"

His hand slid from her hair even as her poor attempt at thrashing finally tossed her tattered slippers off her feet. She spotted one as it flopped onto the dirty concrete now behind him a heartbeat before her sexy kidnapper bent them both forward. She realized with a start he was ducking them into the car she'd seen moments earlier. He didn't seem to care about her struggling as he twisted himself sideways and set her on a long, plush leather seat. He paid no mind to the driver whose head she briefly glimpsed. He simply set her down, reached over her shoulder, and pulled the seat belt around her in one smooth motion. Once that was clicked into place, he snapped the door shut and settled in his own seat.

"Home," he said, tone sharper than she'd heard it, his gaze darting forward only for a second.

"Yes, sir," the driver said as the engine rolled over.

Harmony was too stunned to find her voice for several long, precious seconds. *You have got to be kidding me.* It wasn't until an actual privacy screen began sliding up between the diver's cab and the larger rear space containing her and her kidnapper that she finally snapped into motion. Or, at least her mouth did.

She twisted as much as her seat belt would allow and let loose. "What is the matter with you? You can't just kidnap me like this! And in broad daylight? No way no one saw that!"

He looked amused, which did nothing to make him less appealing. Damn him. "Yet no one tried to stop me." His amusement fled as soon as the words left his mouth. "I've hardly kidnapped you. You were fleeing. I'm helping you flee faster, and with less damage to your inadequately protected feet."

"My—" She stopped herself before she could repeat his ridiculous words. "You can't be serious."

His expression settled into something she could only define as hard. "Deadly."

Harmony dragged in a breath, attempting to keep herself focused and calm. "If I'm not kidnapped," she said, trying to speak at a respectful level, "then let me out."

"Anywhere you need to go, I will take you."

She frowned. "That's not the same thing. Why

should I trust you? Why should I not assume you want to hurt me the same way he did, or worse?" If worse was possible. She did have her doubts.

His expression darkened and he reached out, pulling one of her arms into his hand. She stiffened, yet his touch was surprisingly gentle as he ran his fingers over her forearm. Over the exact spot where Ricky had gripped her before she'd finally broken free. "I will not harm you," he said. "You will learn to trust me, Harmony. And you will tell me the story behind your panic today."

Some stupid, naïve part of her wanted to trust him. It was a feeling she couldn't explain. She had to draw yet another deep lungful of air—air that smelled much more like him, which didn't help—to remind herself that she couldn't. She was on her own. Even her parents had betrayed her. This stranger had no obligation, no *motivation*, to do anything other than take from her.

Harmony pulled her arm from his warm and faintly calloused touch, noting he offered no true resistance. Of course, he had her belted into the back of his vehicle. She couldn't exactly run.

"Believe it or not, I'm used to being locked down. So if you're banking on me caving to some messed-up Stockholm syndrome, you picked the wrong woman. You're better off to just let me out."

A low, rumbling growl emanated from him. "Add that to the list of things I want to hear about sooner than later."

Well, she would admit to herself, that wasn't the response she had expected. *He's playing me.* Harmony folded her arms across her chest and scooted to put her back against the corner of the seat, for what distance that managed to create.

"You want me to spill my entire life story to some

stranger who just grabbed me up off the street? Why, exactly? Do I look that stupid to you? I don't even know your *name*, I didn't actually run into you, and despite what you said, you've yet to let me out of this car. I don't know what you want, but you aren't entitled to some kind of compensation from me, so chances are you're going to be severely disappointed."

Infuriatingly, his face transitioned back to visibly amused for a lingering second. The expression softened the edges of his eyes, giving them a warmth she could easily appreciate. If she were in a position to appreciate him. Then he propped an elbow onto the back shelf behind the headrest between them, the motion tilting his body slightly toward hers, and he said, "Zeno Darkhan."

Harmony stared at him, her mind not processing his strange words. The subtlest hint of an accent flared in his voice when he had spoken that time, too faint to identify but adding to his allure. *Allure I am ignoring.* She pursed her lips and repeated what he'd said to herself. "Is that your name?"

He inclined his head. "Yes. And to answer the rest of your accusations, I do not take you as stupid, nor do I have any ill intentions toward you. Whatever you're running from, Harmony, you are safest with me. But I cannot remedy your problem without knowing what it is, so no, I have not let you out of the car. Nor will I, while you have neither a destination nor proper footwear."

She scoffed before she could stop herself. "*You* cost me my footwear!"

He arched a brow. "Those worn-out slippers were little more than tissue paper." In a fluid movement he bent forward and pulled both her feet up onto his lap, physically twisting her sideways on the seat in the process.

Harmony let out a yelp in surprise. "What are you

doing?"

Zeno curled both hands around the tops of her feet, just shy of her ankles, and squeezed gently. "Making sure you aren't bleeding, Little Dove." He moved his hands up the length of her feet in a caress she would have called tender under any other circumstance. His mesmerizing gaze had dropped to her feet as well, and despite the angle he'd given himself, he didn't seem to be making any effort to sneak a peek up her skirt.

Harmony squirmed, her face heating as his fingers moved around to her exposed soles and her weakness was revealed. Her feet were horrendously ticklish. "D-don't!"

Zeno chuckled, the sound low and rumbly. She could feel the vibration of it through her legs and it sent a very different vibration through her body. He continued gently sweeping his fingers over her feet, even inspecting her toes and rubbing her heels, before finally dragging his gaze back up to hers. "It seems I owe those flimsy slippers of yours an apology. They at least did their job."

She wasn't sure what sound she made, or even how to describe the feeling as it crawled up her chest. It was somewhere between a laugh and a sigh, blended with a gasp of relief. "You … you really…" What she wanted to ask sounded so stupid, and *felt* stupid, but it needed to be asked. She licked her lips and tried again. "You were really just checking to see if my feet were okay?"

Zeno inclined his head, rubbed one thumb across the inner curve of her ankle, and gently returned her feet to the floor. When he straightened, and after she had resituated herself, he met her increasingly confused stare. "I will never lie to you, Harmony."

Warmth blossomed in her chest for no reason whatsoever. She pushed her face into a frown despite the feeling. "You expect me to believe that?"

He didn't blink. "I hope you'll allow me the

opportunity to prove it."

She should have anticipated that response. Then again, she could never have anticipated any of this—any of the events of the afternoon. So Harmony replayed everything Zeno had said to her since their surprise encounter, searching for a single clear contradiction. The only thing she could find was the whole possible-kidnapping thing. And something inside of her insisted she consider that he'd been gentle with her at every turn. A fantastic deception, or proof of his claim? *He asked for an opportunity.* She'd lost her mind if she was even considering believing him, but she wasn't sure what more she had to lose.

Consciously uncrossing her arms in an effort to not exude such shut-off body language, Harmony posed a theoretical question. "So, if I asked to go to the airport?" He had said something about her having a destination, so making the scenario specific seemed more sensible.

His brow twitched almost imperceptibly. "I would insist on a detour to acquire you new shoes," he said, tone calm.

He's really hung up on that. "But you would take me to the airport?"

"Yes," Zeno said. "I would take you to the airport."

Harmony studied him. "And you'd let me go into the airport? Board a plane of my choosing?"

Another whisper of a smirk teased his lips, just for a second. "I appreciate your cleverness, Little Dove. And yes, I would."

She warred with herself on whether she should believe him. His responses seemed sincere, but how well could she really trust her own judgment? She pushed the concern down. There was another question she needed to ask. No more theoretical crap. It was easy enough to pass those tests. "Then … why?"

One of his dark brows arched up his forehead again.

Harmony made a vague sweeping gesture to the cabin of the vehicle surrounding them. "Why all this? Why give a darn about me? Why the pledge of eternal honesty?" *Okay, phrasing it like that makes it sound a little dramatic.* But he had said "never."

Zeno made a sound like a muted sigh. "It might be too soon for that answer, Little Dove."

She frowned. "So you won't lie to me, you'll just straight up refuse to answer."

He held her stare with faintly narrowed eyes. "Tell me this: did you run from the vermin who put his hands on you because of what he *did*, or because of what he *is*?"

The breath lodged in her throat and Harmony's eyes blew wide. She barely registered the sensation of the car coming to a stop. Her heart leapt back into overdrive as a new realization rushed through her. This man who may have kidnapped her or may have deluded himself into thinking he was her rescuer was like Patrick Eades. He was a shifter.

She knew they existed outside of her neighborhood, she wasn't that ignorant, but she'd let her guard down anyway. She hadn't considered she would somehow run into one once she'd put that comparatively small section of New York behind her. She was a fool.

Chapter Three

She was a human. Of fucking course his mate was a human. It was no wonder he hadn't found her yet in all his travels. The beautiful, tiny woman whose scent had slammed into him like a fortified castle wall looked barely old enough to drink by her government's standards. Yet, for a long moment, as Zeno had stared at her on that sidewalk, he'd wanted nothing more than to drop to his knees and drown in her. He remembered hearing that dragons knew their mates immediately. He'd always wondered if it was a scent thing or some intuitive line-of-sight awareness, and having experienced it, he still wasn't sure he could explain.

It was simply everything.

She was everything.

Harmony. Human, petite, cautious little Harmony. She was notably smaller than him even in his human form, though she had enough meat on her to grab hold of. Or sink his teeth into. Preferably both. She was fucking stunning. She would have been regardless of what she wore, with her wavy blonde hair and sky-blue eyes over pale, easily marred skin and all those curves. The tight dress she wore only emphasized all of that.

It was hard to think straight with her scent surrounding him, with the feel of her soft skin under his hands and the melody of her voice in his ears. But he hadn't lived over four centuries without learning a thing or two about self-control, so Zeno managed not to succumb to his baser instincts before they even reached his penthouse. Which was not to say the feat was easy.

Their banter had helped. He genuinely wanted to know everything she would share of herself, but most critically why the stench of misplaced vermin lingered on her skin. Specifically over a bruise that had just started to form. She wouldn't surrender her secrets so easily, however. He was conflictingly proud of her for that.

As the car rolled to a stop, Zeno asked a subtle-enough but nonetheless loaded question that brought their progress to a screeching halt.

It was a hurdle they were going to have to overcome, sooner rather than later, but that logic did nothing to soothe him as the scent of her fear skyrocketed. It overtook her confusion and any beginnings of relaxation she had developed in an instant, surging higher than it had even when he'd hauled her off the sidewalk without warning and piled her into his car. He forced himself to watch as she again retreated to the far corner of her seat, as if the extra half-foot would insulate her.

There was no use, then, in asking whether she knew of shifters in the general sense. He hadn't had to explain his verbiage. She knew what had put that mark on her arm.

Zeno barely bit back a growl and all but ripped off his seat belt. He would track down the honey badger whose stench was associated with that bruise and burn it to ashes for touching her, for scaring her. But first he needed to know precisely what the rodent had done—just in case he needed to make it a slower death.

More importantly, he needed to make certain his mate hadn't become so frightened that she feared all shifters as a species. That would be a rather significant problem.

He managed not to slam his door as he climbed from the car, then raced around to her side and pulled her door open. She wasn't expecting him and let out a short squeak as she began to topple backward. Zeno caught her swiftly, leaning around her to release the seat belt and making sure it didn't snag on her anywhere before he lifted her from the car. She was stiff in his arms, her breathing shallow. The fear held steady in her scent.

Agitated as much with himself for causing her distress as with the existence of it at all, Zeno bumped the door shut with his hip and turned toward the partially lowered driver's window. "I'll call if I need anything more today. Do not speak of this."

"Of course, sir."

Zeno twisted away from the car and strode toward the private elevator. The sooner he got Harmony tucked away where they could talk, the better. He couldn't risk bumping into any of the building's wayward residents, let alone any of his local associates, until he had at least assuaged the fear that almost paralyzed her. If that fucking badger was responsible for this reaction, he would make it beg for death.

He managed to angle his thumb out enough to press it onto the screen reader that unlocked the elevator, and the box was rising toward its destination before Harmony finally shifted, however slightly, in his arms. Zeno dropped his gaze to her, unsurprised to find her arms still folded over herself and her eyes still too wide.

She looked away from the steadily increasing digital display and met his stare again. "You ... said you wouldn't hurt me."

He dragged in a breath and did his best not to growl when he spoke. "I will not, Harmony."

The dip in her brow would have told him how little she believed him if her scent weren't already conveying that information loud and clear. "Then what do you want with me? Why did you haul me off the street?" Tears built in her eyes and her hands shook in a tremor that worked its way through her entire body. "Are

… are you going to send me back to him?"

Zeno locked his jaw to keep from roaring his fury at the tangible tang of her fear, and the sadness that underscored it.

The elevator settled on his floor and he strode out, grateful to be released from the box he hated having to use. Another awkward twist of his thumb later, and his interior door unlocked enough for him to shove inside to the main space. His penthouse was three stories tall in some areas, though he had portions of enclosed spaces on the second and third level as well. But he'd wanted something potentially large enough to at least curl up in if for any strange reason he should need it. Though height was only one factor, and with the necessary encumbrance of furniture, there was no getting around how uncomfortable it would be if he ever had to put that height to use.

The truest reason he insisted on penthouse living—at least in big cities—was, of course, for the sky access. And if he'd been in this mood for any other reason whatsoever, he would surely have already been ripping out of his clothes and stretching his wings.

This time he couldn't. This time, no matter the freedom and release it usually provided, flight was not the solution. Not immediately.

Zeno carried his frightened human mate into the main sitting room and lowered to a knee to set her gently on the well-cushioned sofa. Letting her out of his embrace was the last thing he wanted to do, but he recognized it was necessary for the time being. His touch was unwelcome. Still, even knowing that, he couldn't stop himself from dropping a hand to cover both of hers as their gazes clashed again. "I will say it as many times as you need to hear it, Little Dove. I mean you no harm." He gave her hands a faint squeeze. "The vermin who left that bruise on your arm will never lay another finger on you. Not while I breathe. But I would very much like to know that story, and if that's why you're so frightened."

Her breaths were shaky and her muscles tight, but Harmony made no attempt to tear from him and flee. He'd sort of expected her to, so he supposed that was a start.

Raging against his instincts, Zeno pulled his hand from her skin and took a step back, moving to claim the opposite corner of the sofa he'd set her on. There was a single cushion between them. It felt monumental, but he forced himself to hold his position.

Harmony lowered her gaze, still struggling with herself. It wasn't until she moved her hand to rub at her bruising arm that he realized where she was looking. Quietly, she said, "You don't seem like … them."

Zeno scowled. "Them?" Was there a whole clan of honey badger shifters in New York and he'd somehow *not noticed*? They weren't exactly common, let alone in the Americas. He nearly snorted at himself. He wasn't one to talk on that front.

Harmony dragged in a breath, moved both hands to curl slightly into the fabric of her distractingly tight skirt, and lifted her head to let her gaze drift out the window wall. "The gang of shifters who run the neighborhood where I grew up. You don't seem like them."

His scowl deepened, alarm bells ringing loud in his head.

"It's just that I've … never met any others." The tears returned to her eyes and the scent of her fear became punctuated with a trace of salt. Her lips trembled for a beat and she hurriedly wiped at her face before finally turning her tortured stare to him. "They're bullies. Monsters, on the inside. It's like living in another world.

They demand protection money and insist everyone in the neighborhood treat them with reverence. If they show up for dinner, we give them food. If we barely have enough to feed ourselves that night, too bad, we still have to feed them. If we don't cooperate with one of their demands..." Her voice trailed off and she folded her arms around herself.

Zeno rolled his jaw as understanding lit slowly inside him. He couldn't stop the low growl from escaping—didn't even think to try—until he saw Harmony's eyes get big again.

"I-I'm sorry," she said, ducking her gaze. "You probably don't care. Or don't want to hear about that."

Zeno propelled himself forward and caught hold of her chin, tipping her head up with thumb and forefinger. He curled his other fingers into the back of the sofa to keep from hauling her bodily onto his lap. "Just the opposite, Harmony. I *do* care. Where you're concerned, I care more than I can put into words. I want to hear everything. Tell me every fucking detail. Every offense, every struggle, every triumph." He stroked his thumb over her smooth skin. "Tell me the name of the insignificant honey badger that touched you, and who his alpha is. Tell me where I can find the bastard." He paused, sucked in a breath, and whispered, "Tell me what I can do to earn your trust."

Harmony stared at him, shock working its way in through the fear. He watched her swallow, heard her heart slow to something closer to normal before leaping into a faster rhythm again, and waited as her lips parted. She reached up, moving slowly at first, and cautiously pressed her fingers against his wrist. She seemed to gain confidence when nothing happened and pushed his hand from her chin. He allowed it, because he'd known he shouldn't have touched her again so soon.

Her hand immediately fell back to her lap and Harmony said, "I still don't understand what you even want with me. How can you ask me to trust you when you do all this? How can you expect me to trust you when for all I know you just want to *eat* me?"

Yet another angry growl clawed at his throat. He knew damn well she didn't mean that the way he would if he'd made the suggestion. "Are you saying that vermin—"

"He's a violent, murdering monster," Harmony said, her voice suddenly filled with fire. "And he isn't even the worst of them. He's just the one who kept sniffing after me, the one I could never get away from. So today, when my parents decided to hand me over to him like some game show prize, I finally ran. I just literally ran out the door in a panic. I don't even know how I got away. I wouldn't have if he'd had any of his friends with him—the wolf is fast, I've seen that guy move before. But today I was lucky. Today Ricky came by himself, like he really thought I'd just go along with that." Tears spilled down her face as she paused for breath, her voice cracking. "At least, I thought I was lucky, but now here I am, grabbed up by another shifter. So, what do you want with me? Are you going to eat me? Rape me? Dissect me? All of the above?"

This time Zeno didn't fight the growl as it rolled up his throat and vibrated past his lips. He could feel his blood heating with his anger. He understood a little better now, and that understanding was going to be a very bad thing for more than one of his shifter cousins.

He knew, vaguely, of a group of mismatched shifters who had set down roots in some small section of New York. They had banded together some decades prior and carved out a section of the city for themselves, much the way wolves form a pack and stake a territory. Since their establishment they hadn't drawn any egregious public attention, so the larger shifter populous had let them be. For the most part, shifters as a species tended to abide by a "live and let live" philosophy whenever possible. They were as similar to each other as they were different, and most of them respected that. Zeno, for one, typically appreciated it.

Except in this instance. In this instance, his mate had been threatened, and no self-respecting dragon could let that go. Neither could he afford to make handling that situation his priority.

Willing the fire within him to settle again, Zeno released a slow, almost steam-free breath. "I will deal with that threat, Harmony," he said. "More importantly, I want none of those things." His lips curled despite his best efforts. "I will eviscerate anyone who ever threatens you in such a way." He wanted to properly answer her question, but he feared she wasn't mentally ready to hear the words. "Though I will allow you a say in the fate of your parents. After we've fully discussed the situation."

Her mouth dropped open. "Allow me—" She leapt to her feet. "They're my parents!"

Zeno nodded. "Precisely."

"Don't 'precisely' me." She shot out a hand and snatched up one of his couch pillows, swinging it at his head without warning. She continued to smack the pillow into his head and shoulders as she shouted, *"Don't— just—sit there—threatening—my—parents!"*

Zeno finally reared back, reached around the useless weapon, and caught her flailing wrist in a just-firm-enough hold. "They bartered you off to a man who would have raped and likely slaughtered you. If you were lucky. And they did so knowingly."

Her blue eyes sparkled with unshed tears as she glared defiantly at him. "They're my *parents*." Despite the look in her eyes, her voice cracked with her words, the pain too deep to hide.

He gave a light tug on her arm, toppling her onto his lap and causing her to lose her grip of the pillow. Then he banded an arm around her back, cupped her face in his other palm to hold her startled stare, and said roughly, "And you are my *mate*."

Her wet gasp rattled his soul as she gaped up at him. Her chest heaved with a hard breath. "I'm … what?"

Zeno brushed some whisps of blonde off her forehead and let his fingers glide over her smooth, quickly reddening cheek. It took more than a little willpower not to drop his gaze down her exposed throat and see if the blush faded there, or extended down to the tantalizingly low neckline of her dress. He wanted to know—he wanted to know so many things—but he had to wait. She didn't even trust him yet.

Making sure to hold her wide-eyed stare, Zeno gentled his tone and said, "You, Harmony, are my mate. The predestined partner I have been searching for."

The breath rushed from her and she gave a hard shake of her head, dislodging his hand before she finally started to squirm in his hold. "No. No, I definitely am not." She shoved free of him, stumbling several steps away this time before turning to face him again. "*Mate*? I'm not an expert on all that, but there's no way a guy who looks like you and has resources like you obviously do would choose a poor, sheltered, fat girl with nothing to her name. Like, *nothing*." She motioned down herself. "This stupid dress is worth more than I am, okay? So whatever your angle is—"

Zeno shoved to his feet and stepped into her space, planting his hands on her hips before she could run. He held her firmly in place, barely enough space between them for a heaving breath, and said lowly, "The next time you so much as imply that this scrap of fabric holds more value than you, I will tear it from your body, rip it into shreds, and set every one of those shreds on fire. One by one." He let his grip tighten, just a little. "As for the rest of your self-image, Harmony, let me tell you how we fix all of that. If you've been sheltered, I will show you the world. You can explore anything and everything you desire, learn languages and trades to your heart's content. Or you cannot, if you so choose. If my wealth is a problem for you, I'll cast it off. No fortune in the world is more valuable than a mate. And as for your perceived difference in our *looks*—"

He bent down, lowering his lips to her ear, and pulled in a lungful of her scent. "When I say you look delicious and I want to eat you, I'm not talking about dinner. I mean, all I can think about is burying my face in your pussy, your thighs locked around my head, and feasting on your sweet nectar until your legs give out. I look forward to sinking my teeth into your thighs, your hips, your shoulders, and your fucking perfect breasts. Not to take a bite, but because I want you to feel the raw passion the mere sight of you rouses in me. Your body is temptation made flesh, Little Dove, and I do not intend to share."

She was trembling again, her breathing erratic, but this time he could smell the distinct aroma of her arousal fighting with her lingering fear. The fear itself had lessened considerably. Both were good things, but the fragrance of her arousal was a distraction Zeno wasn't sure he could handle. Perhaps he should have held his tongue somewhat.

Harmony lifted a hand and pressed against his chest, pushing hard enough to prompt him to straighten and lighten his grip. Her eyes were confused and glossy. "Why ... why would you choose someone like me? You don't even know me."

Zeno offered her a small smile. "Our match is fate, Harmony. Our souls have been assigned to each other since we came into being." He lifted a hand and brushed his thumb over her cheek, beneath her eye, as one of her tears attempted to leak free. "I will give you time to get to know me, and I hope to learn everything about you. But the one thing I already know—" He curved his hand behind her head, letting his fingers thread her hair as he pulled her closer. "You are the one I have been searching for, and no matter how long you ask me to wait, I will not walk away from you. From us."

She set both hands on his shirt, her fingers curling in the fabric. "You would wait?"

"Yes."

Harmony swallowed visibly, rolled both her lips between her teeth, and a distinct tension settled in her shoulders. As if she were bracing herself for something. "I feel kind of overwhelmed with all of this, and today in general, but ... I can't really run away from home like this." She dropped his gaze to glance down at herself, and her expression was sheepish when she looked into his eyes again. "Could you—or do you know someone who could—come with me back to my parents' house?" She licked her lips. "I can't expect to get anywhere with just a dress. I don't even have a way to call someone. But I'm afraid ... I'm too scared to go back on my own."

Zeno released a slow breath and leaned in, allowing himself to press a kiss to her forehead. She wasn't screaming, panicking, frozen in fear, or trying to run. She wasn't agreeing to hide away with him and bare their souls, let alone bond them, but it was still a start. Any step forward was better than where he'd been the day before. "I'll go with you, Harmony. But I would like to know a little more about that situation first. And you still need shoes."

She let out a bark of laughter and slumped completely against him. "Seriously, do you have a foot fetish or something?"

Warmth bloomed through him at the feeling of her voluntarily pressing against him. For as used to the various intensities of heat—inside and out—as he was, this feeling was new. And he liked it. It was hard to resettle his hands at her hips, harder still not to seek out her skin with his lips. "I have a driving need to protect you from harm. The streets of New York are hardly a place to be walking barefoot."

Harmony tilted her head into his chest in a failed attempt to muffle her giggle, then straightened and pointed toward the window and balcony beyond. "Says the man with a massive, movie-style balcony like thirty stories in the air."

Zeno grinned. "Wait until you see what I do with it."

Chapter Four

Harmony stared at the tablet Zeno had handed her after she was resettled on his unreasonably comfortable sofa. She had a basic sense for how the device was supposed to work—it wasn't like she didn't watch television—but holding the tiny computer in her hands was surreal. Not only had he handed it over to her without any word of caution, he'd said something about giving her a minute to browse and then walked from the room. She could hear him, faintly, in the direction where she'd glimpsed the kitchen.

Her hands remained frozen on the sides of the device as she drank in the vivid color on the screen. She processed the periodically cycling presence of an ad at the top of the displayed page before her brain finally recognized different shapes and styles of shoes. Women's shoes, categorized for her to choose from, or perhaps scroll through. She wouldn't know without touching the screen. But before she could unlatch one hand to do as much, her gaze caught on the website logo at the top.

Harmony's stomach rolled, dropping to the floor. *Holy crap.* She'd done a poor job of making herself heard before if he thought she could even afford to look through the windows of that store!

"Do you have any food allergies I should know about?" Zeno called as her mind reeled.

Harmony carefully set the tablet beside her on the sofa and twisted enough to look toward the kitchen. From across the penthouse, the kitchen had seemed large and almost imposing with its predominantly dark aesthetic, but with Zeno in it she changed her mind. It suited him. Which was a ridiculous thought to have. She watched him stir what looked like iced tea, just for a second, before blurting, "Can't I just go to Wal-Mart?" The idea of walking through any store as she was less than appealing, but she had to be reasonable. She could pay him back the cost of whatever she needed from Wal-Mart. Presuming her parents hadn't torn through her room and found her small stash of funds.

Zeno turned to face her, setting the spoon he'd been using onto the counter, and a frown bent his lips. "Why would you want to go there? Did nothing appeal to you at—"

"There's no way I can shop there!" She made a stupid gesture toward the tablet he wouldn't be able to see from his angle. "I don't have a job, okay? My parents would never voluntarily let me work, so searching has been hard. I've sent out like one email resume so far and I don't have a lot of hope for that." It'd been over a week and she hadn't heard back, and the job listing was gone. She blew out a frustrated breath. "I couldn't pay you back for something from somewhere so expensive in a *year*. I could pay you back for some cheap flip-flops from Wal-Mart when we get to my parents' house."

Silence stretched for several long seconds as Zeno studied her. Then he turned toward the fridge, putting his shoulder to her. "You didn't answer my question."

Harmony blinked. *His question?* "Um, sorry, could you repeat it?"

He pulled open the refrigerator. "Do you have any food allergies? I don't want to keep anything in my home that will hurt you."

Her mouth moved on autopilot as confusion held her frozen. "Shellfish."

"Shellfish," he repeated, as if to himself. His head tilted marginally to the side, the angle drawing her eye to where his hair was loosely restrained behind his shoulders. His hair looked like it should have been wild, like it was permanently windblown, yet it barely shifted with his movements.

She found herself wondering if it was soft to the touch or coarse and stiff with product, her confusion and previous flustered frustration momentarily forgotten.

Then Zeno straightened, knocked the fridge door shut, and twisted in place with a single package in hand. He said nothing as he strode through the kitchen, cutting straight for the window wall and with what looked like barely a press of his fingers stepping onto the balcony beyond.

Harmony slid the feet she'd curled beneath her to the floor, curious about his actions and about the surely breath-stealing outdoor space. Why would he have taken something from the refrigerator out to the balcony?

Her curiosity was immediately answered, and her forward momentum stalled, when Zeno gave a flick of his wrist and tossed the package into the air. Of course, it caught on the wind she could see tugging at his clothes and hair, but that ceased to matter a heartbeat later. The mysterious package of food was barely higher than his head and tumbling outward—possibly downward—when a very bright, unexpected burst of orange-red fire sliced through the open air.

Harmony clapped a hand over her mouth.

The fire blinked out, leaving only the faintest traces of dark gray smoke to waft up into the sky. The package was gone, entirely incinerated. She was as certain as she could be, though she hadn't seen it happen, that the fire had come from Zeno.

The man who called himself her soulmate had somehow magically generated fire to obliterate something he could easily have thrown away. Or donated. For the life of her, all she could think was she hadn't known shifters could do that.

Zeno stepped back inside, pulling the glass door shut once again behind him, and retraced his path to the kitchen. He stopped at the sink to wash his hands, then re-entered Harmony's field of vision as he rounded the far side of the sofa, carrying two glasses of iced tea. "I wasn't sure how you preferred it, so I made one each way." He set the glasses onto the coffee table and indicated one. "This one is without sugar."

Harmony forced herself to keep her breathing steady, absolutely certain he could hear her heart pounding regardless, and licked her lips. "With, please." She appreciated that he hadn't assumed, or taken the liberty of deciding for her. Or she would appreciate it, probably, when she could think about anything other than the stream of fire he seemed to have so casually generated moments ago.

Zeno obligingly passed her the sweetened tea before reaching for the other. He watched her over the rim of his glass as he took a long swallow, but didn't speak until he'd set it down again. "Did that frighten you?"

She choked on her own, coughing roughly to clear her throat and holding tighter to the glass. "Seeing fire suddenly appear in the air like that? Yes. Of course. I don't know what type of shifter you are, let alone how you did that, but I am a very *burnable* human." Officially the most ridiculous thing she'd ever felt compelled to say. "For that matter, what were you even doing? Why dispose of food that way? If it was bad, toss it out or something."

His brow pinched, just for a second, before his expression settled again closer to neutral. "I apologize for startling you. That was a package of lobster. It seemed better to incinerate it than to risk poisoning you."

Her heart faltered. She'd watched him immediately dig through his refrigerator, but it hadn't seemed realistic that he would do something so drastic in response to what she'd said. Feeling a strange combination of guilty and flattered, Harmony said, "You didn't have to—I mean, you could have just eaten it."

Zeno made a sound like a disgruntled huff. "There may be any number of reasons you choose not to kiss me in the future, Harmony. Because I've knowingly eaten a food to which you are allergic will never be one of them."

Heat rushed through her and Harmony was sure her face had gone a bright shade of pink. That wasn't nearly as scandalous as the last suggestive thing he'd said, but she wasn't used to being spoken to that way. It was somehow both embarrassing and thrilling. She lifted her tea to her lips in a poor attempt to hide her face, took a small sip, and quietly asked, "What about the … fire?" She wasn't aware her gaze had dropped to the coffee table until he answered her, until she realized she couldn't see the smirk she was sure she heard in his voice.

"Dragons breathe fire, Little Dove. I promise you I have excellent control."

Her head whipped around so fast that even the minimal movement made her dizzy. "You're a *dragon*?"

Zeno inclined his head. "Yes. And I'll show you my other form when you're a bit more comfortable with the idea." His gaze dropped to the tablet before he reached out and lifted it from the cushion between them. "Of course, all of that is presuming you can decide on a pair of shoes. Do you have any concerns with this store other than the cost?"

Harmony tried not to gape at him, her mind ping-ponging to keep up with and process the conversation. The man was way too calm for what he'd just revealed.

She had known shifters existed all her life, but never once had she heard that *dragon* shifters were a real thing. Not to say she'd investigated it. Any historical records on shifter ancestry were not easily acquired, as the general existence of them was not as widely known as she had thought when she was younger. *But still!* She pulled in a breath, flexed her fingers around her glass, and dug up some type of response to his latest question. "Do I need another concern?"

Zeno hummed low in his throat and lowered the tablet once more. "So we have to discuss the money issue first, then."

Her brows flew to her hairline. "What?"

Wordlessly, Zeno reached out and plucked the slippery glass from her grasp, setting it onto the coffee table in front of her. Then he scooped up her nearest hand and pulled it across the space between them, folded between his. His warm amber eyes burned out at her, the steadiness in them somehow keeping her calm even as her heart rate spiked again. When he spoke, his tone was equally patient and gentle yet somehow strong and unyielding. "Perhaps you misunderstand. I am not offering you a loan. I fully intend to buy these shoes for you as a gift. The first of many." He gave her hand a light squeeze. "Take advantage of my wealth and let me spoil you, Little Dove. You may choose whatever you like."

Harmony swallowed hard. The heat of his touch surrounding her hand felt almost overwhelming, yet it was nothing compared to the intensity of his stare and the weight of his words. "That's ... a lot, Zeno." She didn't really mean the shoes, although at the price that designer charged, the statement was still true.

His lips lifted in a small smile that made his eyes light up like the flame of a candle, warm and somehow inviting, and he adjusted his hold on her hand to raise her knuckles to his lips. Without taking his eyes from hers he pressed his lips there in a chaste, lingering kiss. The action sent a thrilling tingle down her spine that was warm and pleasant, and felt more than a little indecent with the way the sensation dropped into a coil low in her belly. That, and the look in his eyes, reminded her of the more scandalous things he'd whispered in her ear earlier.

The things she'd only read about in the books she'd borrowed from one of her classmates well over a year prior. She hadn't realized there were men who actually talked like that.

Definitely not the time to be thinking about those kinds of things!

Zeno recaptured her hand after pulling it from his lips, squeezing again. "As I told you before, Little Dove, all I ask for right now is a chance. Give me a chance— give *us* a chance—and you will understand this is simply my nature. I want to take care of you, to see you not only protected but comfortable and thriving. I hardly think a pair of good shoes is too much."

Tears rushed her eyes without warning and Harmony found herself curling her fingers around the hand beneath her own.

Protected. Comfortable. Thriving.

Her parents had worked incredibly hard—too hard—on one of those things, in arguably all the wrong ways, up until that day. Or they'd made it seem like they had. But the others? No one had really made an issue of the others. The others were … unimportant.

"Harmony?" Concern laced Zeno's strong voice and he leaned forward, removing one hand from hers to reach for her face and gently wipe away a tear that had trickled down her cheek.

She licked her lips and shoved down as much of her roiling emotions as she could. "I'm sorry, I … I'm not used to…" It was too humiliating to even put into words and her throat constricted. Instead, she indicated with her free hand for the tablet. "I'll look for some shoes, if it's okay." Maybe he was right. Maybe one pair of nice shoes was okay. The smile he offered her before again handing over the tablet certainly said it was.

When she saw the prices attached to the shoes, she nearly gave up all over again. Add that he'd already declared his intent to pay extra for expedited processing and to pay a third party for delivery—a service the company didn't offer—and Harmony felt ill. She opened the URL to take herself to a cheaper alternative, but the weight of Zeno's stare over her shoulder kept her from seeing the plan through. So she thought she'd prove her own point instead, and dutifully shopped for the most appealing pair of shoes she could find.

Of course, she found so many options it took her several minutes to narrow them down again, and ultimately, she added two pairs to her cart—one pair of irresistible ankle boots with a low two-inch heel that were super cute and more fashionable than she'd ever been allowed, and one more practical but still girlie sandal. He had said he wanted to spoil her, after all. Once the cart was ready, she turned the tablet to face him with the predicted price on the screen.

"There isn't even an option on the website for the expedited thing you mentioned, so I can't begin to guess how much extra that will add to the total," Harmony said. "I really don't mind looking somewhere else." Her mother would have beat her over the head for even suggesting spending so much on shoes.

Zeno took the tablet, scrolling briefly to examine her choices. "Only the two?"

Harmony felt her eyebrows climb up her head. "Did you see that total?"

"Harmony." He looked over at her.

She scrunched up her lips, just for a second, before nodding slowly. She wasn't sure why he was so dead set on this when he could just as easily drive them back to her neighborhood and have her retrieve the shoes she already owned. "Two is plenty."

He inclined his head, tapped at the screen, and proceeded to dig his phone from a pants pocket. His thumb rolled across the smaller device as he sent a message somewhere, then he set the phone down and swiped at the tablet again before repeating the same process. After which, he set both devices on the coffee table and turned to face her.

"Your shoes should be here by hours' end. I'll take you home to get anything you want from your parents' house and talk things out with them after that, and when you're done, we can go to dinner."

Needing something to do with her hands, Harmony reached again for her iced tea. "That ... I mean—" She sighed. "Dealing with my parents could take hours." She gulped some of her drink. "You don't have to stick around for that." She certainly didn't recommend it.

Zeno's brow furrowed. "I'm not abandoning my mate to face confrontation on her own," he said firmly. "Let alone in such a dangerous place." His voice hardened unexpectedly as he spoke. "If any member of that gang shows up to try and take you, I'll make sure they regret it."

Her breath faltered in her lungs. The truth was, she expected Ricky would come sniffing around if she was there too long. And she expected she'd be quite literally locked away the moment she re-entered that house, until her parents felt motivated to let her out. The only way she would ever taste freedom again was if Zeno were with her to make sure of it. But that seemed like far too much to ask.

Her gaze dropped to the space between them, space she knew he'd given her for her own peace of mind. Space some irrational part of her suddenly detested.

Harmony removed one hand from her glass to wipe at her face before she'd even realized more tears had rolled free. "I'm not free," she whispered, unable to lift her gaze. "That's why I had to run. That's why … that's why I can't get a job. That's why I had to sneak my way through college—which is not easy, let me tell you." She choked on a bitter laugh. "I was never allowed to date, I only have like one friend and we're not super close because my parents don't approve of her." She finally dragged her gaze back up to his patient, scowling face. "I don't know what their arrangement with Ricky was, not specifically, but they won't approve of you, either. Because you weren't their choice." Her mouth opened to say more, but when she heard the next words forming in her brain, her throat constricted again.

Her parents wouldn't approve of Zeno, first and foremost, because he *valued* her.

Zeno reached out again, brushing his fingers over her cheek before cupping the side of her face in his larger palm. Though his fingers were faintly calloused and his hand was strong, his touch remained gentle and warm. And the fire in his eyes … she couldn't define it, but it didn't scare her. Not at all.

"You are strong, Harmony," Zeno said, his voice almost rough despite the low tone of it. "I have many words I might like to say to your parents, but the most important thing is that you hear me now. It does not matter what they demand or expect. You are your own woman. Your choices are your own. Whether you choose to take a job and be solely dependent upon yourself, to stay with your parents and endure their rules, or even to embrace a life with me—the right to make those choices is yours, and yours alone." He stroked his thumb across her cheek. "Do you understand?"

The life she had known so far, that had led to her being handed over like a prize to a disgusting excuse of a man, or the dream she had been nurturing for the past few years. Or ... a different dream, so unlikely she'd never really dared to imagine it at all. The impossible ideal of a life of warmth and happiness, with affection and comfort, and possibly even respect.

Harmony trembled as she set her glass back on the table. It seemed too unlikely to seriously consider. She reached up and covered the back of Zeno's hand with her own, her eyes seeking his. "I want to know more," she whispered brazenly, "more about you, and of what could be."

What he offered seemed crazy, but it would be stupid to throw away such a chance without at least looking into it, right?

VOLUME TWO

Chapter Five

The sun was setting by the time they rolled up to the curb in front of the single-story home Harmony had grown up in. She'd managed to forget her nerves for a precious little while, up in Zeno's magnificent penthouse, but the familiar sight of her childhood home brought the twisting, nauseating feelings rushing back. She had been so desperate to get away when she'd fled, she hadn't truly considered the consequences, let alone if fleeing was a viable option.

Her parents were going to be furious.

Zeno's hand settled on her shoulder, drawing her attention away from the sight through the window. "We can still leave. You don't need to face this today if you're not ready."

Harmony attempted a smile. They'd talked for close to two hours, about all sorts of things, and even though she knew it was crazy, she felt as though she knew him much better. Enough, for certain, that she knew he understood her anxiety and reservations for more reasons than because he could smell them. In whatever ways those feelings were smellable. And in turn, she understood his offer was genuine—they had only come there at all because she had insisted, and they would leave if or when she changed her mind.

That knowledge gave her strength. It made her smile easier. "This will just get harder the longer I put it off."

Zeno's hand slid to the nape of her neck, his touch warm enough to raise her body temperature. "I won't leave you to face this alone, Little Dove."

The warmth at her neck coursed through her

chest. She opened her mouth to thank him, and all at once she realized the other looming danger. It went beyond what her parents would do to her for punishment, or even the threat of her next encounter with Patrick Eades. If this went remotely wrong, she might never see Zeno again. The idea of that was unacceptable, in a way Harmony couldn't explain. Even to herself.

She moved on impulse, not wanting to lose something she'd never truly had. Not wanting to regret the time she'd wasted. She twisted and half crawled across the bench seat of the sedan, pressing herself against him as her hands found his jaw a moment before her lips connected with his. The scrape of his trimmed beard beneath her fingers was like a tangible echo to the low rumble of his responding growl before his arms banded around her and Zeno took control.

His tongue slid past her lips as he tangled a hand in her hair, his other hand gripping the back of her dress. He leaned into her, kissing her deeply, with a hunger that made her entire body burn and clench simultaneously. It was unlike anything Harmony had imagined, let alone experienced. He held her so tightly that both their bodies moved with each heaving breath before the kiss even broke.

When it did, and his grip on her hair loosened, Harmony found herself straddling his thigh and panting in his face. She might have been embarrassed about all of that, if it weren't for the barely contained need shining back at her from his eyes and the way his own chest rose with deep, unsteady breaths.

Zeno smoothed his hand over the back of her dress in a slow, deliberate motion, never taking his eyes from hers. "Be very careful about when you decide to kiss me like that again, Harmony. I can't promise I'll remember my restraint."

She shouldn't have smiled, and she certainly shouldn't have laughed, but it was too surreal. "Should I apologize?"

"No. Never." He moved the hand from her hair entirely and cupped her cheek, thumb brushing her lips.

He didn't add more, and she felt irrationally flustered by that.

Instead, after she could breathe a little easier, Harmony said, "I guess we should get this done." She had used the plural on purpose, but it felt wrong. This wasn't his fight. It didn't have to be his problem.

Zeno exhaled and carefully scooped her off his lap, setting her into a seated position at his side. "Then let's begin." He turned his attention forward as he dropped one hand to the door panel and projected his voice. "This could take some time. Go get yourself something to eat, and return."

Harmony laid her fingertips on Zeno's arm even as the driver voiced his understanding, and when Zeno met her gaze again, she spoke her new concern in a whisper. "Will he be all right?"

Zeno smiled, but this smile was not the warm and encouraging expression he'd offered her before. "Of course. This is my car, and Roland is my driver. In this neighborhood, my scent should be enough to drive off nearly any threat." He held her stare a beat longer, as if to make sure she heard the meaning behind his words.

She did. She recognized she was bringing a freaking dragon to a neighborhood run by misfit shifters who didn't truly have a central alpha, though several of them claimed the dynamic. She understood that the dragon at her side was already riled up, more than any of the other shifters would be, and more than likely his mere presence would stave off the threat of them. Because at their core they were creatures of instinct.

So she put her fears aside—those fears, at least—and this time climbed to her own two feet when Zeno opened her door seconds later. Her cute new boots went surprisingly well with the dress she still wore, and since Zeno had apparently tossed in a pack of socks with her shoe order, she'd opted to wear them.

If she was going to upset her parents, she might as well go all-out with it.

Harmony drew a deep, not-as-steadying-as-she'd-hoped breath, squared her shoulders, and led the way up the short, cracked concrete walkway to the front door. Her nerves were rampaging again by the time she found herself struggling with whether she should knock.

Then the front door flew open, nearly swinging into her face, and her mother stood in the entryway. Her nostrils flared and she planted her hands on her hips. "Harmony Lace, where in the devil's name have you been? Do you have any idea what you've done?"

Harmony swore she could feel Zeno's disapproving exhale at her back, despite that—at least for the moment—he continued to hold his tongue. She held tight to the courage she'd gathered moments earlier. "Do you really want to hash that out on the front stoop where all the neighbors can see?"

Linda's brow furrowed and her stare finally lifted in Zeno's direction. The glare wavered for a second before she dropped the entire expression back onto Harmony and demanded, "And who is this? You run away in the middle of an important transaction, then come home hours later—"

"*Transaction?*" Harmony barely kept from shouting the word. "Dad literally shoved me into Ricky's arms and you just stood there!"

"You weren't moving."

"Of course I wasn't moving," Harmony snapped.

"You know how uncomfortable he makes me, and then after the things he was saying—"

"You're right," Linda interrupted sharply. She twisted to the side. "We should take this inside." Her eyes dropped to Harmony's feet. "Those look new. Be careful taking them off so you can return them."

Harmony found herself hesitant. This was what she'd come out there for, more or less, but suddenly she was unsure.

In her moment of uncertainty, Zeno broke his silence. "The boots are hers. She has no need to return them."

Linda snapped her gaze out again, her glare a bit steadier this time. "I appreciate you returning my daughter home, sir," she said tightly, "but this is a family matter. I hope you'll forgive me for insisting you take your leave."

Harmony stiffened. She'd expected this, but hearing it out loud made the fear worse.

Zeno laid his hand at the small of her back and stepped close enough to warm her with his presence. "I won't be doing that."

Linda's eyes widened. "I beg your pardon?"

"Well, look who decided to come home," a different, unfortunately familiar voice called from behind them. It slithered into Harmony's ears and made the hair on her arms stand up.

Zeno let out a low sound of displeasure and turned so he could see Ricky without losing sight of Harmony's mother. The expression on his face perfectly matched the growl he'd emitted. "You must be Patrick Eades."

Harmony shifted her weight to move again closer to Zeno, not wanting her back exposed to Ricky, but her mother shot out a hand and latched onto her already bruised forearm.

At the same time, Linda said, "What wonderful timing, Mr. Eades. This man only just returned Harmony home to us." Her words were once again soaked in sugar, but she leveled a glare on Harmony that dared her to utter a single sound of objection.

Harmony felt her heart crack. It was as if her mother didn't understand at all.

"Mrs. Lace," Zeno said, something like a warning in his voice.

The metal porch railing squeaked the way it always did when Ricky leaned too heavily against it. "Interesting. It smells to me like the big guy here got a little handsy with my Harmony first." He paused just long enough for Linda's brow to pull tighter. "Did you help yourself to my prize, Grandpa? That's real gross, you know."

Harmony barely heard Zeno's next growl over the thunderous beating of her heart. She'd known coming back would be hard, but she had naïvely thought she would at least get inside before the argument really started.

"You little whore," Linda said in a low, poorly whispered hiss, her lips curling back. "Is that why you ran? Just to spread your legs for someone else?" Her fingers dug into Harmony's arm, the nails biting Harmony's skin.

Harmony stared at her mother, mouth slightly agape. Shock fizzled through her system. "Are you serious?" She tugged on her arm, but her mother's grip didn't budge. So she raised her voice. "You *bartered* my virginity to the neighborhood bully, behind my back, but *I* would be the whore if I had chosen to give it away instead? How dare you!" She surged forward and swung her open palm across her mother's face.

It was enough to startle Linda into rearing back and releasing her arm.

Harmony stumbled free, adrenaline and too many emotions burning through her. "That's so outdated, so outrageous, and so completely unacceptable! *I* decide my life, do you hear me? Not you, not Dad, and not Ricky Eades!"

A chuckle that had never once meant anything good for her carried on the air from somewhere over her shoulder before Ricky said, "You sure about that, Princess? Because I think you might wanna rethink it."

Harmony whirled around only in time to see Ricky's feet leave the ground. Her eyes widened and whatever she might have snapped at him died in her throat as she watched her longtime tormentor tumble end over end down the short stretch of half-dead lawn toward the street. Behind her, her mother gasped dramatically.

Zeno stepped just in front of the porch, almost as if guarding it. "Get on your feet, vermin. This is your neighborhood. Let's see you fight for it."

Ricky released a long, strained groan and flopped onto his back. Seconds passed before Harmony was sure she heard him curse, and seconds more passed before he pushed to his knees. He wiped blood from his obviously broken nose, glaring openly at Zeno. "You're gonna have to challenge a lot more than just me if it's the *neighborhood* you want, old man."

"And I would win," Zeno said plainly, "if that were my intent." He let the words hang in the air. "Consider this instead." He turned a glance toward the porch, looking past Harmony and into the house where she knew her mother still stood, before facing forward again. "Harmony is my mate. You will never come near her, nor upset her again, or I will take great pride in peeling that filthy hide from your tiny, feeble body and setting your corpse aflame."

Harmony watched Ricky's eyes go wide and his face pale, as if he were genuinely frightened.

"Mate?" Linda whispered.

Ricky forced out a hard laugh and shoved to his feet. "You expect me to believe that? You're delusional! That girl's mine, old man! I've been waiting years for her to ripen up, no fuckin' way am I—"

Zeno stretched one arm out at his side and the skin rippled, shimmering under the nearly sunken sun as if it had suddenly become liquid and turbulent. He simultaneously stepped forward, his pace neither slow nor hurried, and in seconds his arm had transformed. Shifted. Probably double the size, flesh replaced by almost reflective blue-black scales, and four long, slightly curved ivory claws at the end of the hand. Or paw.

Linda gasped.

Ricky stumbled back, one foot landing in the street. "F-fuck, you're really a—"

Zeno suddenly leapt forward, his shifted arm swinging, and dirt, dead grass, and small chunks of shattered concrete flew into the air as Ricky threw himself entirely into the street. A trail of short-lived fire chased him until Ricky's scampering feet hit the sidewalk on the opposite side.

"O-oh my God..." Linda said in her most scandalized tone.

Ricky ran to the other side of a parked pickup, leaned halfway around the hood of the truck, and shouted, "Fuck you, old man!"

Zeno straightened, his arm doing the shimmery-rippling thing again as it shifted back to familiar bronze-colored flesh.

Harmony only then realized she'd lifted a hand to her chest while she'd watched. She'd never been one to crave violence, let alone to hope anyone would fight over her. But she couldn't deny there had been … *something* appealing in whatever had just happened. She did her best to push down that feeling for the moment and pivoted on her heel to face her still slack-jawed mother. "You know what? I don't need to come in. I think we've said enough." She waited while Linda refocused on her. "I would appreciate it if you would at least tell Dad I said goodbye."

Linda's mouth moved, but no real sound came out.

Harmony turned and stepped off the porch before Zeno could rejoin them. At his arched brow, she drew up the strongest smile she could manage and said, "I don't want to be here anymore, and I don't really want to think about the fact that I don't have anywhere else to go. Can we grab that dinner?" Not that her appetite would last long once she started thinking about the meaning behind what she'd just said.

Or why her arm hurt again.

Or the show Zeno had just put on for half the neighborhood to see.

Or how stupidly sexy it had been.

All those things were their own problems. Well, most of them. If she could delay thinking about problematic things long enough for one more good meal, that would be great.

"I forbid it."

Harmony blinked, her eyes tracking the way Zeno's attention lifted from her to focus on something over her shoulder while her brain scrambled to process the words. Her mother's words. She twisted in place, keeping Zeno close at her back, and saw her mother striding toward them with a look of fury on her face. "What?"

"I forbid it," Linda repeated. "I will not allow my daughter to go gallivanting around with some monster clearly old enough to be her father!" Her arms swept wide. "Do you have any idea what will happen to us if I let you go through with this, you selfish, impulsive child?"

Harmony opened her mouth, but the sound of ripping fabric caught her attention and the next thing she knew she was surrounded by darkness. Only the faintest light crept in over the top of the black, leathery shroud that had wrapped around her. It wasn't until she registered the sight of an ivory, claw-like protrusion running along the top outer ridge of both sides of her new enclosure that Harmony realized what had to have happened.

Zeno had extended his wings—also the source of the ripping sound she'd heard—and folded them around her. Probably. They were so large they layered over each other, and obscured her completely, blocking any useful line-of-sight. Of course, it didn't help that she was short by most standards. Zeno's strong arms wound around her middle and he pulled her back to his chest, the wings sliding faintly with the movement. At the center where they intersected, Linda's head became partially visible, and Harmony realized she'd been tuning out her mother's ranting. Not exactly for the first time.

"*Harmony* will decide her future," Zeno said in a low, firm voice that vibrated through her. "If you wish to be her mother, I would advise you to do a little self-reflecting before we meet again."

Zeno moved his hands as Linda sputtered in outrage. Harmony could picture the flustered flush burning brightly on her mother's cheeks—for the moment she continued to think about it at all. Then Zeno had her spun around, an arm around her shoulders, and he swept another beneath her knees. His wings snapped out, jarring a startled shriek from Harmony's mother, and the breath rushed from Harmony's lungs as he used those wings to propel them upward.

Oh my God! Harmony latched her arms around his neck, barely able to see over his shoulders as her mother and the yard grew smaller beneath them. The entire street fell beneath them as he twisted in the air with a single flap of his massive wings, the buildings sliding past almost too quickly to identify. *We're flying. We're really actually flying!*

He lowered them to solid ground at the edge of a familiar circling of trees, and Harmony watched as his wings folded in on themselves before disappearing entirely in another fleshy ripple. No one shouted, nothing caught fire, and no militia of armed men burst from the tree line as Zeno gently set her back on her feet. He let his hands settle on her hips, keeping her close, and watched her as if waiting for a response.

She had so many it was hard to grab hold of one. Harmony dragged in a breath and let her fingers trail over his shirt. "I used to dream of flying," she confessed on a whisper. "That was ... wild. Amazing. Totally reckless, but exhilarating." Her brain was starting to re-engage and she was sure they shouldn't have done that. She blinked up at him with wide eyes. "Will you get in trouble?"

He smiled slowly and his grip tightened. "For that short little jump? Hardly." Zeno leaned in and pressed his nose to the crook of her neck, then his lips, before murmuring, "There are still places in this world we could go where I could truly take you flying, if that was something you wanted."

She was never going to catch her breath if he kept doing things like that. Instead of lecturing him, she curled her fingers more into his shirt. "Really? I ... I might like that. Someday." Some people went skydiving. She apparently went flying with a dragon.

Just one. Just mine.

The thought made her throat close and Harmony stretched her arms around him as best she could. Even though he was leaning down, he was just ridiculously tall. "Zeno."

"Hmm?"

She managed to slip her fingers into his hair and let her eyes close, the scandalous truth escaping her. "Can we go back to your penthouse? I don't think I want a fancy dinner. We've done so much talking ... I want to do something else."

Chapter Six

How Zeno managed not to lose control of himself at the park while they waited for Roland to retrieve them was beyond him. His own adrenaline had been up even without Harmony's suggestive request. The idea that she was going to let him touch her, to be her first? It made him want to roar with pride.

They talked quietly in the car, mostly about how her return home had gone worse than expected. He kissed her hand when the salty scent of her unshed tears hit the air. There wasn't much he could do to reverse the wounds her mother's words and choices had inflicted. He had to hope he could find ways to help those wounds heal.

Zeno bade Roland good night once they reached the parking garage, helped Harmony from the car, and ushered her again into the metal box that would take them up to his penthouse. As soon as the elevator doors closed and the machine began to rise, Zeno pulled Harmony up to him with an arm low around her waist.

She smiled, her cheeks a bright pink. "Do you mind that I'm still…?"

He smirked. "A virgin?"

Harmony nodded.

Zeno brushed his fingers through her dusty blonde hair, letting them trail down the back of her neck where the dress left her exposed, and rumbled, "No, Little Dove." He dropped both hands down low, hooked her thighs, and hauled her up as he backed her into the wall until her legs were positioned around his hips. A soft gasp left her, but he didn't wait for her to speak. "To be chosen as the man who helps you through your first experience is an honor." He slid his hands up beneath her skirt, until his fingers sank into the flesh of her ass.

Harmony latched onto his shoulders.

He leaned closer, torturing himself with the building scent of her arousal, and moved his lips to her ear. "Are you certain this is what you want? To give your body to me tonight?"

"Yes," Harmony breathed as the elevator came to a stop. The faint jostling caused their bodies to rock together, grinding his unavoidable erection against her center, which in turn drew a sharp, delicious gasp from her lips.

Zeno stepped from the wall, snapping a hand back to her knee to encourage her not to release him, and strode to his main door. He held her to him with the hand still on her ass, her arms having curled around his neck, and got them inside the penthouse in seconds. Then, for just a singular moment, he hesitated.

He wanted her scent everywhere. He wanted to show her every pleasure. But it was her first time, it had to be right. Threading the hand not holding her up into her soft hair, Zeno tilted her head back and slanted his lips over hers. He pushed his tongue into her mouth, pulled her hair tighter, and let a low growl of approval vibrate through him when she shoved her fingers into his own hair. Her nails scraped over the back of his neck and his scalp teasingly.

He sucked her tongue into his mouth and ground against her once more before forcing himself to break the kiss. The scent of her arousal had intensified, overwhelming anything else and nearly driving him mad. He could easily have pushed her against the nearest wall and shredded both their clothes, but that wasn't the experience he wanted to give her. So he held himself together long enough to carry Harmony up the stairs, into the main bedroom, where he tipped them both forward onto the large mattress.

She gasped his name at the impact but did not let go, instead pulling him closer for another kiss. "More, please," she said against his lips.

He chuckled, adjusting enough not to crush her with his weight, and indulged her in a long, wet kiss that had their bodies rolling together until he was dangerously close to embarrassing himself. He wasn't even sure he'd mind, if it was what she wanted. But he needed a more thorough taste of her, so he broke from her sweet, swollen lips and licked his way down her flushed and too-tempting throat. He kept his fangs to himself, but he made sure to leave other marks that would linger on her beautiful, pale skin.

Harmony was tugging awkwardly at his shirt by the time he was low enough to sweep his tongue over the top swell of her breasts.

He lifted his head only enough to find her glazed-over eyes. "Did you need something, Little Dove?"

"Too many clothes," she said with surprising urgency. "We're wearing too many clothes."

He smiled. It would mean retreating from her delicious body for a minute, but he couldn't deny her when the end goal was so mutually satisfying. "So we are." He angled his head to lick a stripe up her neck, nibbled at her chin, and murmured, "Do not get up from this bed. I'll strip you myself."

Her flush intensified and her chest heaved, and she unlatched her ankles from the small of his back. "Okay."

Zeno released her properly and pushed to his feet, took an extra second to extract and silence his cell phone, and proceeded to shed his clothing. The shirt was tossed toward the garbage bin, already ruined from having shifted enough to release his wings, but the rest was kicked aside. He assumed from her lack of experience that he was the first naked man Harmony was seeing, at least in person, and he interpreted the way her blue eyes widened and raked over his body as confirmation.

If he had any luck at all, he would remain the only man she ever saw naked.

Harmony pushed up to her elbows as he stepped toward her. "Um. Wow…"

Zeno lowered to a crouch and set to work removing her new boots and socks, chuckling as he did. "You aren't going to ask if it'll fit, are you?"

"Would that really be an unreasonable question?" The words came so quickly he guessed he'd hit the proverbial nail on the head. She let out a self-conscious laugh. "I know it's cliché. It's just … you're … and it's not like I've ever, you know, had anything up there before."

Zeno set her footwear off to the side and stood swiftly, keeping himself between her legs and letting his hands sweep again under the skirt of her fitted dress. A dress he now understood she hadn't chosen for herself and was less than comfortable in. "We are fated, Harmony. There's nothing to fear. I will take care of you."

She was having trouble meeting his eyes—which his ego didn't mind in the least—and she pulled her lip between her teeth. A flicker of nerves edged into her scent.

Zeno moved a hand to cup her cheek, guiding her gaze up to his and holding it there. "We can stop at any time. Just say the word."

Harmony released her lip and offered him a smile. "I don't want to stop."

He sensed only confidence and certainty from her, so he nodded, brushed a kiss over her lips, and dropped his hand. Without asking her permission or offering warning, Zeno gathered up two fistfuls of the dress and ripped it off her body. He wasn't in the least surprised at her startled half-shriek, though he was a bit impressed that she didn't reflexively pull away.

"Zeno! That was my only outfit!"

He swept away the last threads and let his eyes rove over her nearly revealed form. The black panty and bra set wasn't fancy, but it was slim and intentionally low-profile, all of which meant her breasts were barely held in place and there was hardly enough fabric between her thighs to cover what mattered. The best kind of torture, until he considered that these, too, she had been forced to wear before being handed off to another shifter. He'd just have to buy her replacements.

Aloud, he said, "You hated it."

"Yes," she said carefully, "but it was my *only* outfit. I definitely can't go out like this!"

A low growl built up in his chest and Zeno reached out, running his palms over her smooth, bare skin. "No, you cannot." He saw her eyes widen, so he went ahead and finished the thought. "I would have to massacre any man who saw you so exposed." To emphasize his point, he ran his thumbs over the waistband of her panties.

She shivered, a soft gasp escaping her. "That— that's not the point."

"You'll wear something of mine until more clothes arrive for you," he said. His hands continued up, over her abdomen, palming her soft belly and perfect skin. "I have more than enough, it's fine."

"I-I can't just—" Harmony groaned when he peeled her bra away and caught her breasts in his palms. Her breathing faltered.

He squeezed and molded the plump flesh,

watching her luscious, pale tits spill out of his hands as his mouth salivated for a taste. The woman had more curves than was healthy for a man's sanity. And her nipples were such a beautiful dusty rose, so perfectly centered and already hardened with desire.

"Z-Zeno," she said, all but whimpering, as he dragged his thumbs over her nipples.

He grunted low and divested her of her bra, then guided her back down onto the bed. "I'm going to taste every perfect inch of you, Little Dove." He didn't give her more warning before letting his mouth descend on one of her breasts, licking and sucking his way around the skin while he kept the other occupied with one hand. He blazed a trail to her nipple and pulled the entire areola into his mouth, teasing her rosy bud with both teeth and tongue.

Harmony began to squirm and moan, her hands lifting to claw at his arms.

Eventually, he switched his attentions to her other boob and gave it the same thorough treatment before finally lowering his kisses to her torso. It seemed the blush disappeared at her bosom, he noted, and the feral side of him loved having discovered the answer to that curiosity. He kissed, licked, sucked, and massaged his way down her body, letting his mouth and hands roam, and groaned as the aroma of her arousal only grew. He was painfully hard, but he willed himself to ignore that for the time being. For as much as he wanted to bury himself inside her and feel her come apart around him, he needed to give her a taste of that pleasure first.

And a taste was precisely what was on the menu.

Her panties went flying over his shoulder when he finally reached her hips and Zeno stroked his hands down her thighs. He swept his gaze back up her body from where he knelt on the floor at the edge of the bed, barely able to see her face from the way her chest heaved. "I'm going to taste you, Harmony. I'm going to do exactly as I said earlier and feast on your sopping wet pussy until you scream my name. When it comes, don't fight it. Let yourself feel it."

She rolled her head to the side in an attempt to see him without otherwise moving. "You're really going to—"

In answer to her question, Zeno bowed his head and swept his tongue between her folds. Her natural musk exploded on his taste buds and he groaned deep in his throat, his hands digging into her hips as he lost himself in his mission. He licked everywhere his tongue could reach, swirled it around her opening, and retraced his path back up to her clit.

Harmony thrashed below him, moaning and gasping intermittently.

He sucked her clit into his mouth and pushed a single finger into her channel. Her body went stiff for a moment before her breathing changed, telling him she was close. So he eased off her clit and pumped with the finger a couple of times before inserting a second, and when she still seemed primed to shatter, he squeezed in a third. One suck at her clit with the three-finger pumping had Harmony's back coming off the bed and a choked-off cry of release dragging from her throat.

Zeno eased his ministrations slowly, his balls throbbing as if her orgasm had nearly triggered his own.

Harmony was splayed on the bed, her hair already a mess and her chest heaving, as he pushed up from his knees. "H-holy ... that was..."

Zeno crawled over her, trailing one sticky finger up her chest as he moved, and met her hooded gaze. He lifted his two other fingers. "Taste yourself on me."

She blinked at him, her focus sliding to his

fingers, and stared for another second before opening her mouth in invitation. So he stuck his fingers inside, pushing all the way to the knuckles. Her lips closed and her tongue slid over his skin and they both groaned.

He pulled his fingers free before his impulse could backfire. "Do you need to stop?"

"What?" She frowned faintly. "Stop? Why?"

Zeno shifted his weight and dragged her up the mattress, landing himself between her thighs once more, and reached down to curl one hand around his aching dick. "Because next is the main event, Little Dove. So if you need to stop, now's the time."

Her eyes tracked his movement as he rolled his thumb across his tip and she licked her lips. "No," she whispered. "No stopping." Her gaze snapped up to his. "I'm still sure."

He growled and slammed his lips to hers, crushing her to the bed and rocking his hips against her pelvis. Her arms curled around his back, fingers pressing into his skin, as she kissed him with equal fervor. He was going to lose his mind, but if it was like this, that was fine. Better than fine.

Zeno broke from the kiss enough to reach between them and line himself up at her entrance, her pussy spread open and soaked just for him. It was a fucking glorious sight. He needed to remember to be gentle and not plow into her.

"Zeno, please," Harmony begged, squirming as much as his renewed hold on her hip allowed.

He met her eyes again and pressed the tip into her opening. "No stopping." He pushed forward, moving slow, gritting his teeth against the instinct to rut into her sweet body like an animal. When she gasped from the sting of inevitable pain, he lowered his lips to her skin and kissed her everywhere, from her abdomen all the way up to her panting lips.

By the time their tongues slid together, he was fully seated inside her tight, never-before-fucked pussy.

Mine.

Not necessarily yet. She hadn't agreed to that. But he would be damned if he'd ever let another man touch her, let alone set her free.

Harmony broke the kiss on a ragged gasp as he dragged his cock out to the tip, her arms curling around his shoulders. She startled babbling his name like a mantra and he took that as a good sign.

Zeno reached down, hooked her legs by the knees, and bent them up over his arms. The angle enabled him to sink deeper and he growled against her skin, fighting the urge to let his fangs sharpen. He pulled his own lips over his teeth to keep himself in check and picked up the pace, knowing there was no way he'd last as long as he would like the first time they were together. Probably that was also for the best.

Her hands tangled in his hair, scraping at the back of his neck, as he started really thrusting into her. Her pussy was already convulsing around him, so Zeno rolled his hips and let himself nuzzle into the side of her neck for a lingering second. She smelled so fucking good. She was so small. She was so goddamn perfect. Her smooth, soft, mostly unblemished skin was heaven against his rougher flesh.

She shouted his name as her orgasm neared again.

He lifted his head enough to growl in her ear, "Fly with me, Little Dove." He needed to feel it. Had to hold out at least that long.

Her whole body spasmed a second before she let loose a scream of pure, undeniable ecstasy, her back arching beneath him and her pussy clamping down on his cock.

Zeno tipped his head back and roared, letting her pleasure pull him over the edge. He held himself above her for several long seconds even after his dick had poured out everything it could. He was still half-hard, still sitting inside her, but she would be sensitive and exhausted after her first time.

He gently lowered her legs back to a natural position and eased himself out of her, unable to fully contain the scowl at the sight of his seed spilling from her immediately after.

Harmony made a tired humming noise and rolled her head. "Zeno? Something wrong?"

Smoothing his expression, Zeno stretched out for a moment to lay beside her and brush some wild whisps of hair from her face. "No, Little Dove. Nothing at all." He pressed a kiss to her forehead. "Are you all right? I need you to tell me if I pushed too much."

Her lips lifted in a smile. "I'm exhausted," she said, "but in the best way. I'm pretty sure it's not supposed to feel that good the first time."

He chuckled and tipped her chin up to catch her lips for a short, not-so-chaste kiss. "Clearly it *can*, if your partner does his job right." He kissed her one more time. "Let me get a towel and clean you up before we sleep." He should insist on feeding her, but if she was tired, he wouldn't make her get out of bed.

Harmony caught his arm in a loose grip. "Exactly how familiar are you with popping cherries?"

Zeno stared at her. "With what?"

She pursed her lips, another blush staining her cheeks. "I'm not dumb enough to think you've lived hundreds of years and never had sex, but ... you're not actually just a virgin collector or something, are you? You promised you're single..."

Zeno frowned and settled at her side, his hand

automatically finding her skin and gliding across it. "Harmony. I am not nearly so devious. Yes, I've had sex in the past. Though not in many years. It's not quite the most driving urge when you've lived for a long time and you know the one you seek is not available." He let that linger for a moment. "It's been much longer since the last time I bedded a virgin. Probably not since I was a wild youth who didn't care so much about settling down."

She twisted a little, putting herself half on her side, and laid a palm on his jaw. "Promise?"

He leaned forward and pressed his forehead to hers. "I swear. Though I am interested in where this concern stems from."

Harmony let out a sigh and dropped onto her back once more. "I guess there's a part of me that still can't figure out why a crazy sexy guy like you would look twice at a girl like me. Especially if you've lived for hundreds of years. I'm like a baby in comparison. A fat, ugly baby."

Zeno growled, scooped her up, and rolled them over until she was sprawled atop his chest and his hands were half-fisted in her hair. Her eyes were wide again and blinking rapidly at him. "You are fucking perfect, Harmony Lace. But it would never matter to me what you looked like. *I'm* the lucky one. You're human, you don't have the ingrained instinct to find a specific mate. You could have dismissed me as a match as easily as your mother did—as being too old or otherwise unqualified." The words stuck in his throat, because she still could. She hadn't accepted him yet.

Harmony scoffed. "You do own a mirror, right? You really don't look 'old' by the standard definition." She stretched out a hand and trailed her fingers through his hair, near where he knew the silver was the thickest. "It's distinguished." Despite her words, her brow furrowed almost immediately and something like hurt washed over her scent.

Zeno opened his mouth to ask about it, but she didn't let him.

Harmony pulled her hand away and pushed at his chest until he eased his grip, letting her up, letting her slide to his side. Her brow was still pinched and her shoulders tightened, like she wanted to curl in on herself. "You … you didn't claim me."

Chapter Seven

Harmony felt irrationally, unacceptably exposed as the reality slammed into her. Despite his heartwarming words and searingly wonderful touches, she'd given him a chance and still Zeno hadn't chosen to claim her. She didn't understand. He had insisted he'd been searching for some obscene amount of time, *hundreds* of years, for his one predestined mate. He had insisted that was her. Yet he hadn't claimed her.

She watched his lips dip into a subtle frown and her breath lodged in her throat as she waited for his response.

"Of course I didn't." His words may as well have slapped her straight across the face.

Harmony began shaking her head and pushed further away from him, doing her best to keep the tears at bay. *Of course he didn't.* Did that mean he'd lied all this time? Had she been a fool for even considering what he'd been saying to her? A fool so desperate for escape from her cage that she'd fallen right into his trap?

"Harmony," he said, stretching out an arm as if to catch her. To stop her.

An option that was somehow even worse whispered in the back of her mind. Maybe he hadn't lied at all. Maybe every word had been true, but the afternoon they'd spent together—and seeing her body unwrapped and exposed as it was—had convinced him he didn't need her. She wasn't good enough.

Her feet nearly slipped over the beautifully polished hardwood floor as she made a dash for what looked like his bathroom. Her body was tired and she was humiliatingly nude, but she didn't know what else to do.

Where else to go. It wasn't like she had a home to go back to. Or even a hotel. Hell, she no longer had *clothes*.

She choked on a sob as she clicked the lock into place, ignoring Zeno's voice on the other side of the door. The sturdy thud of his fist—she assumed—connecting with the door was a little harder to ignore, but he didn't break it down. Though he certainly could have.

She stumbled away from it and dropped onto the toilet, but even once she'd cleaned herself up from that she still felt wrong. Exposed, sticky, uncomfortable. Disgusting.

I'm either the world's biggest fool or so repulsive even my fated mate doesn't want me.

"Harmony, I can smell your tears through this door," Zeno called again. His voice was louder and sounded angrier, rougher, than she was used to. "Don't think for a second I won't tear this door down. Come out here and let me explain."

Her hands balled into fists, anger helping for a moment to stifle her pain. She shouldn't be hurt. She'd been used. She was being tossed aside. What she ought to be feeling was outrage. "Just give me space!" Her gaze swept over the spacious bathroom, searching for anything she could use to her advantage. She wanted to step into his luxurious-looking shower and soak until her skin was raw. First, she needed to be sure she would get the opportunity.

"Harmony, I don't understand—"

She slid open a drawer and found a pair of trimming scissors. They would have to do. Plucking them from within, she shouted, "Leave me alone or I swear I'll plunge these scissors into my wrist." It sounded horrible and a part of her questioned whether she could go through with it.

But would that be so much worse than continuing

to be used?

The air itself felt heavier in the silence that followed. Then, quieter, Zeno said, "You wouldn't really … Harmony, please don't do that."

"Then don't make me!" She stood there for what felt like several minutes before she heard another sound from him. It almost sounded like shuffling.

"I've set towels by the door. I'm going to change the bedsheets and leave some clothes for you on the bed, but I'll be downstairs. Out of your way." Another momentary pause, and something in his voice changed in a way she hadn't heard before. "Please just let me know when you're ready to talk."

Talk? She bit her tongue to keep from shouting at him. She wasn't sure she believed he was really just walking away. But then, if she was right on either of her theories, she was giving him the perfect excuse to get rid of her, too. So maybe he was.

Harmony waited until she was reasonably certain he'd left, then set down the scissors and tiptoed to the door. She pressed her ear against it, heard nothing, and cracked it open. All she found were two fluffy, dark blue towels, neatly folded and stacked directly beside the door. She scooped them up and scampered back inside her improvised shelter.

The towels went on the sizable counter, then she finally took herself over to the unreasonably large walk-in shower. Even if they showered together, there would be room for more. Not that they would. She would leave this room eventually and never return.

The thought made something inside her ache sharply. She shoved the pain as far from her mind as she could and started twisting knobs until she figured out the setting she wanted. When the water was hot, Harmony stepped beneath the spray, tilted her face up, and let herself cry.

It was like releasing the gate on a dam. In seconds she had collapsed to her knees, her body shaking beneath the spray from the onslaught of her tears. She wasn't even sure why it was as upsetting as it was. Sure, it was humiliating and insulting, but she was crying as if he'd broken her heart. She sort of felt like he'd broken her heart. It made no sense. Even if he'd been telling the truth about their destinies, she was human, and he hadn't claimed her. His rejection shouldn't hurt as it did—right?

Harmony had no answers. She couldn't organize her thoughts well enough to think past how badly it hurt and much she just wanted to be wrong.

Everything had been perfect up until she'd come to that horrible, gut-wrenching realization. He'd been wonderful with her. The perfect combination of gentle and passionate. She had honestly not truly believed sex could feel so good—she'd thought it was a fantasy written about in romance books specifically *because* romance books were escapist fantasies for women. It wasn't like she had anyone she could ask. It wasn't like the one guy she'd let kiss her on one of the rare days she'd been on a college campus had made her feel anything remotely like what she felt when Zeno made any sort of contact with her. There was no comparison.

He doesn't want me. That was all there was to it. She was only hurting herself by thinking about anything else. By lingering.

Zeno had taken her innocence, perhaps hoping he'd feel more drawn to her than he did or perhaps because he thought he was entitled to it, she didn't know. But he had no intentions of keeping her heart. He was an ass for that, probably, but she wasn't blameless, either. She'd asked—begged—for his touch. She only hadn't known the ultimate outcome.

Harmony gasped, realizing she had turned and slumped against the tiled wall of the shower as water continued raining down on her. She had been too desperate, too naïve, and too optimistic.

She looked down at herself, at the way her belly fat squished with her position and her breasts hung sloppily down her chest. The way her thighs splayed out like pale slabs of meat. It was no wonder he hadn't wanted her. She was fat, short, and in every way an unsuitable match for a man as imposing and powerful as Zeno Darkhan. She was a freaking *ant* compared to him, and she hadn't even ever seen his other form.

Tears and shower water burned her eyes and she was having to breathe through her mouth, as her nose had become congested due to her sobbing. She needed to pick herself up and start the scrubbing process before the water got any cooler. She needed to suck up her pride and pilfer whatever clothes Zeno had left out for her so she could leave this place, these memories, and this future that was never meant to be behind her. Except every time she thought about doing that, the tears redoubled.

She blamed her exhausted hyper-emotional state for why she didn't notice that her privacy had been invaded until it was too late.

Without warning, Zeno's shadow blocked out the bathroom light and his low, displeased growl filled the room. A single second later, she was up and off the floor, his already familiarly warm, strong arms supporting her like she weighed as much as a paper doll. "No more crying."

Her muscles tightened and she sucked in a wet, watery breath. She didn't have the strength to shove at him. Not when he twisted them enough to switch off the shower, not when he practically stomped from the large shower stall, not even when he set her carefully on her feet again. He kept a hand on her hip, kept her pinned between himself and the bathroom counter, and snatched the top towel off the stack.

"I—" Her words were lost as the towel descended on her and Zeno set to work rubbing at her skin. She tipped her head back and closed her eyes, trying not to just be a crying mess.

"We're going to talk about that reaction you just had," Zeno said, his voice quiet and rough. "But I'll explain myself first."

"Y-you don't ... have to," Harmony said, her voice choked as she pushed the words out through her constricted throat. The last thing she wanted was to hear him articulate the things she'd already concluded.

Zeno exhaled heavily, the air heating around them. He slid the towel between her legs with swift, tender efficiency, then dropped it and reached for the other. With the other he wrapped up her hair and squeezed, then caught her chin and encouraged her to meet his gaze. "I didn't claim you because you hadn't asked me to."

Harmony sucked in awkward breaths, trying to figure out his words. Trying to figure out where they fit in with what had happened. "So it *is* my fault."

He arched a brow. "There's no shame in needing time, Harmony." His fingers trailed along her jaw until his hand was curled loosely around her neck.

"Time." She sniffled, not even feeling awkward about it, and finally found the strength to at least raise her arms and cover her breasts. "Time for what? Do you want me to take the time to make myself prettier? Lose weight, learn about makeup, until I've fixed the ugly parts? I'll always be short. Time won't change that."

Zeno growled and hauled her up again. He carried her from the bathroom, dropped her back onto the bed, and laid himself over her body. He dragged her arms up, holding them above her head by the wrists. His chest pressed into hers. "I told you I would never lie to you. You are the most beautiful, tempting woman I have ever laid eyes on. I will worship your body for every day of my life if you give me the chance. *If* you change yourself, you do so only because it is a change you personally and strongly desire. In which case, you will always have my support. In every decision you make—every decision that does not involve self-harm—you will have my support. Even if it hurts *me*."

Her heart slammed against her ribs. She wanted to believe him.

Why was he saying these things now? He'd had such a perfect opportunity to let her disappear from his life. She was so confused.

And she still couldn't breathe properly. She gasped—for breath as much as from the impact of Zeno's words. "I thought ... I thought you were saying ... you didn't want me."

Pain and sadness flashed across Zeno's face and he adjusted his weight, releasing her wrists in favor of leaning down and pressing his forehead to hers. The position rested his pelvis more heavily onto her, making her keenly aware of his straining erection. "Little Dove," he said, a yearning slipping into his voice that hadn't been there previously, "I want you more powerfully than I have ever desired anyone or anything in all my life."

Taking advantage of having been released, Harmony reached down and found his skin with her hands. She threaded her fingers in his hair. Part of her felt as though she should have been pushing him away, but all she could do was hold him closer, to the best of her ability. "You said—" She hated the way her voice and her breathing was messed up with her congestion. But she ignored it. "You said 'of course not.'"

Zeno's brow pinched, for a split-second, before he sighed again. He angled his head to press a kiss to her cheek. "I would never claim you without your explicit consent, Harmony. You hadn't given that. So, *of course* I didn't. That's all I meant."

This time she did try to push him away, tugging at his hair and only succeeding in prompting him to push up to his elbows. He still hovered over her, covering her in his body heat and reminding her that he was as naked as she was. "I asked you to take me."

"You asked me to be your first," he said, speaking calmly. "You never said a word about tying your soul to mine. You never said you had decided to see out the next millennium at my side. You asked for sex."

She opened her mouth to argue his words, to insist she had meant it another way, but his unflinching, patient stare held her retort at bay. She knew she'd expected him to claim her. And she knew, when she replayed the moments leading up to their return to the penthouse in her mind, that even as she'd asked him to make love to her she hadn't been sure what she was asking for. She wanted him, without question. She wanted to know his touch and his kiss. She had been absolutely sure she wouldn't regret letting him be her first.

She didn't think she had given any real thought to soul bonding or living for as many as another thousand years. That probably meant she hadn't said the words.

Harmony licked her lips. "So if I don't say it clearly, then you won't … ever?"

Zeno's jaw tensed for a moment, but he leaned in, bowed his head, and brushed his nose up the length of her throat. She felt his chest rise on a deep inhale. Then he pushed himself up again enough to meet her gaze. "Not without your sober and explicit consent. Ever."

She stared at him, trying to get her brain to work right. Trying to understand what he'd just done and why it had made her skin tingle with delight. But it was hard to think about anything when she couldn't breathe, so finally she pushed at his shoulders. "I can't breathe," she gasped.

Zeno rolled off her immediately, pulling her up to a sitting position and sweeping her hair from her face. "I'll be right back." He disappeared into the bathroom, returning with a small box of tissues, and detoured to the garbage bucket before bringing both up to the side of the bed. He held out the tissues. "Here. I can make you some peppermint tea if that would help."

Embarrassed, Harmony held a tissue up to her nose and ducked her gaze. "I think I just need a moment. Could you maybe pretend not to watch?" Blowing her nose in front of the man who'd just taken her virginity was humiliating. It was ten times worse on the heels of making an ass of herself, and she was rapidly realizing that was exactly what she'd done.

All because she had been too lost in her own tangled emotions to make a decision.

Zeno was still kind enough to move around the room, gathering dirty laundry and scraps of ruined fabric, heedless of his glorious nakedness. Or perhaps that was part of his seduction plan.

She was not so polite as to not stare at his butt for a long second when it came into view.

When her nose was as clear as it was going to get, Harmony finally spotted the simple—but probably expensive—t-shirt that had been laid out for her previously and pulled it over her head. The towel Zeno had wrapped around her hair before had been dislodged with the whole bed-tackling thing, but at least her hair was dry enough not to immediately soak the fabric. She opted not to bother with the gym shorts. She didn't even know why he owned them.

Did shifters really need to go to the gym?

A low grunt drew her attention back toward the doorway and Harmony found Zeno standing there, staring at her. He had finally donned a pair of black sweatpants, slung low on his hips, but the should've-been-thick material did nothing to hide his arousal.

Harmony swallowed heavily and tugged self-consciously at the hem of his shirt, which hung to her thighs. He was so much larger than her. "Should I wear the shorts?"

"No." He stepped forward, moving straight to her, not stopping until her back was against the glass of the floor-to-ceiling window that ran the entire length of the wall behind his bed. The man did like his high views. He raked his gaze over her, his eyes practically burning. "Have you calmed down enough to decide your boundaries, Little Dove?"

Too many thoughts swirled through her head. She was probably tempted for the wrong reasons. Surely, she hadn't known him long enough. So she latched onto that little voice of reason and finally said, "I'm kind of sore." Her hands came up, fingers settling on his firm abdominal muscles. "Probably I should at least let myself rest before I make a big decision. And you owe me an awesome breakfast." She smiled, hoping to show she meant it to be funny, before adding a more truthful statement. "But also, I owe you an apology … so I thought, maybe you could teach me…"

Zeno's breathing faltered, just a little, as her hands dipped beneath his waistband. "Harmony," he said, almost as if in warning.

She smiled, curled her fingers around his thick length, and stroked slowly. She watched his nostrils flare, his chest rise with a deeper breath, then she dropped to her knees and shoved his pants past his hips. She'd certainly never done even this much before him, but she obviously knew one did not give a blowjob with the pants still properly in place.

Somehow, she thought he looked bigger than before as his dick sprang free.

Zeno buried a hand in her still-damp hair. "If this is what you want," he said, voice thick and roughened once more, "then open those sweet lips."

She complied immediately, even sticking out her tongue and sweeping it across his tip.

He groaned. "That's right, Little Dove. Follow that instinct. I want you to lick me, root to tip. Don't be shy."

Harmony swallowed a small flicker of nervousness and leaned closer, letting her tongue make better contact with his cock. She focused on the way he held her and the low sounds he emitted and soon her self-consciousness was gone in favor of heady excitement. Soon her tongue was twisting around his length, one of her hands taking hold of him again as she licked back up to taste the drop of pre-cum beginning to form. She didn't wait for his instruction before opening her mouth more and trying to take him inside.

Zeno cursed under his breath. "Easy. Watch your teeth, Little Dove."

Harmony retreated, licked her lips, and made a conscious effort to flatten her tongue as she went back in. She kept her jaw wide, lips curled close to her teeth like a shield, and after two more tries she had nearly the entirety of his cock in her mouth. She swore she could feel him hitting the back of her throat and fresh tears pricked at her eyes, but his grip had tightened in her hair and he'd emitted a deep, guttural groan that made her own body pulse with need. Somehow it was worth the initial sense of discomfort, knowing she was bringing him that pleasure.

She ran her hands up his thighs, over his abdomen, and finally dug her fingers into his hips as she began to bob her head on his dick. Once she got used to the movement, she went a little faster and started rolling her tongue underneath his length.

He grunted again, bending forward until his free hand was balanced on the glass of the window behind her. "You're doing amazing," he said, his breathing uneven. "If you don't want me pouring down your throat, Little Dove, it's time to pull off."

Harmony pressed herself closer, shoving him as deep into her mouth as she could, and hollowed her cheeks on a hard suck. She felt his cock twitch in her mouth as his hand moved to hold her head in place, and again he let out a loud, thrilling roar of ecstasy—and with it, streams of hot cum shot down her throat. Thick, tangier than she'd expected, and almost too much to swallow, but she was determined to do for him what he'd done for her, so she willed herself to endure. She licked lightly at him as her throat worked to pull down every drop, until Zeno finally tugged her forcefully off his slackening length.

She gasped, relieved for the chance at a better breath and somehow faintly disappointed all the same.

He was breathing hard, chest heaving. His eyes were practically fire when they latched onto hers. "I'll feed you breakfast in the morning, Harmony. And then you're going to be mine. Unless you'd rather I eat you out right now."

Heat flashed through her. She definitely felt a degree of hot-and-bothered, but every time she moved her body reminded her she'd also put it through something new and intense rather recently. "Breakfast would be better."

He smirked and pulled her off the floor, locking her against his chest. "Let me hold you tonight. I promise to behave. I want you to see what it could be like, to choose me. To choose us."

The sensual desire that had flickered in her core bloomed instantly into a chest-warming sensation at his words and Harmony smiled. "I would like that. But you should put your pants back on."

VOLUME TWO

Chapter Eight

Zeno had not been exaggerating.

After waking up more comfortable than she could ever remember, Zeno's strong arms curled possessively around her. They had climbed from bed and made their way down to the main floor, where she had watched her dragon-shifting lover, still shirtless, prepare a mouthwatering feast of eggs, bacon, potatoes, and lightly toasted bagels for breakfast. She felt as though she'd eaten like a queen. He'd heaped food onto her plate and not made a single expression or uttered an off-word as she ate. That in itself was a dream.

Then he'd hauled her up onto the kitchen island, stepped between her legs, and buried his face in her pussy. Harmony was sure she would die of bliss before she ever made it to a shopping mall. She wasn't so sure that was a bad thing. When the orgasm crested over her she didn't even think not to scream, or undulate against his face.

Seconds passed before Zeno stood again, neither of them breathing properly, and his face shinier than normal. "Thank you for breakfast, Little Dove."

She scoffed, too breathless to truly laugh, and sank down onto the island. It was large enough that only her head dangled over the edge. "No fair. You got two breakfasts."

He chuckled as his body heat moved away and she heard the faucet turn on. "If you're implying you'd like a second, I can help you with that. But I'd feel better if we moved somewhere you'd be more comfortable."

Her face turned red as she remembered the sensation of her mouth being stuffed full of him. It ought to have been awkward, and certainly not something someone should crave, but she was definitely willing to do it again. She wanted to see if she could do better, if she could take all of him properly.

She nearly missed his low grunt of displeasure as the water turned off.

Drawing herself out of her inappropriately wandering thoughts, Harmony forced herself to sit up as Zeno turned toward her again. "What's—"

He held a finger to his lips, a wet washcloth dangling from his hand, and his phone to his ear. "I would offer 'good morning,' but it's not like you to call for no reason." He tapped the screen and set the device beside her, pressed a finger against her mouth as if to re-emphasize her need for silence, then promptly dropped down and brought the cloth up between her legs.

Harmony sucked her lips between her teeth to keep from making a sound at the sudden sensation.

An unfamiliar, faintly filtered male voice spoke through the phone's speaker, both working to distract her and make her mildly uncomfortable. The latter mostly with herself when she realized she wasn't as bothered with having Zeno where he was while the phone line was open as she should have been. At least, not until the man's words fully penetrated. "I wish I was calling under better circumstances, but this phone call is a courtesy I'm really hoping you don't make me regret."

He paused just for a moment, but long enough for Harmony's brow to pinch. It almost sounded like he was agitated, or trying to offer a warning. Not that she knew the man with the gruff, older-sounding voice. So she listened and tried not to think about the steady movement of cloth at her center.

"In about two minutes, two of my people are going to be at your door," the man continued. "I need you not to roast them. More importantly, I need you to cooperate so we can all get on with our lives."

Harmony glanced down at Zeno as he pulled away, carefully folded the towel, and wiped what she sincerely hoped was the clean side quickly across his face. She wanted to ask what in the world the stern man on the phone was talking about, but she also didn't want to make herself known to that man.

Zeno tossed the towel in the direction of the sink as he stood. "Care to tell me why you're sending a team to my personal residence first thing in the morning, Scott?" He scooped Harmony up off the counter and set her gently down on her feet without making a sound.

The man Zeno had addressed as Scott let out something like a sigh. "They're in the elevator, Darkhan. Officially, I must be recused from the case due to our association."

Zeno growled. "And unofficially?" He snatched up his phone, lifted Harmony by the waist, and propelled them at a breath-stealing speed across the open space until they were up the first flight of stairs.

Scott's words trailed in their wake. "Unofficially is why I called."

Zeno shoved the phone into a pocket as he set Harmony down in a room on the second floor she hadn't seen yet—which was most of them, if she was honest with herself. The room he'd taken her to was obviously for laundry.

She glanced at his empty hand, assumed the call had ended, and looked up at him. "What's going on?"

"We're about to have guests, Little Dove," Zeno said, his jaw tight with obvious displeasure. He brushed his fingers over her face, pressed a kiss to her forehead, and indicated the machines. "Your panties are in the dryer. Grab them, then hurry upstairs and put on the shorts I set out for you last night. I can't have you parading around in front of others without clothes."

Harmony opened her mouth. Closed it. Blinked once. "My panties."

A brief flash of wicked amusement tipped his lips. "I needed information." He gave her a gentle but distinct nudge. "There's no time to explain, unfortunately. We have to deal with this first."

Harmony pouted, but she remembered Scott saying their unannounced guests were already on their way up. "I still have so many questions. Who are these people that you seem worried?" It took her a moment to figure out which one was the drier. His machines were so much nicer than the ones from the laundromat she was used to.

Zeno was already striding for the door. "The government."

Harmony nearly fell face-first onto the machine she'd been leaning toward. The *government*? That was not an answer! Why would any government group be pursuing Zeno? She managed to pull her nice, freshly cleaned panties from the machine, untwisted them, and was stepping into them when someone pounded on the door downstairs.

Her heart jumped into her throat.

Zeno had seemed familiar with the man named Scott, but it was clear he hadn't been prepared for this. Whatever this was. Did that mean he was in trouble? Was it possible he was going to be forced away? What would she do if he had to leave the country entirely? It wasn't like she had a passport.

Harmony waited until she was sure Zeno was downstairs again, more or less a barrier between her and the government people who felt like invaders, before slipping from the laundry room to scamper upstairs. The shorts he'd directed her to put on had fallen to the floor while they'd slept, but she had a general idea where they were.

The tones of multiple voices barely carried to her, but it was enough for her to know Zeno had opened the door. Something inside her insisted that making contact had started some sort of clock. Whatever was going to happen, the countdown had begun.

All she could do was rush into the shorts Zeno had kindly set back on the bed and hurry—carefully—back down the stairs. She moved as fast as she could, but her mind had plenty of time to panic. Plenty of time to imagine so many ways she was about to be walking into a nightmare.

Did shifters have some kind of Visa system and Zeno's had expired? Was this because he'd flown her like three blocks in a public space the day before? Had one of her neighbors seen him shooting fire at Ricky and this was their way of earning Ricky's favor?

Maybe it had nothing to do with her or him being a shifter. She had to consider that, despite all they had talked through before, it would be a long time before she knew everything about him. Perhaps he had debts, or some kind of warrant, and collecting on those was a more intricate system for men like him. She didn't know much about that kind of thing, outside of how it was portrayed in the movies her father sometimes watched.

None of it made sense, but Harmony had convinced herself this government group had come to deliver the ultimatum of him leaving the country or being chained in some unnamed dungeon by the time she made it to the main floor. Her heart beat wildly and she wanted to simultaneously launch into a rage at the people who'd violated their safe space and just curl up and cry over a loss that hadn't technically happened yet.

She was both relieved and concerned to discover Zeno had not let their intruders past the entryway. He stood with his bare back to the open space of his own home, arms at his sides, facing the people whose profiles she could barely see and therefore barring their path. From her angle, it looked like they'd brought some kind of large package or suitcase with them, which was set on the floor.

"I understand you have to investigate those claims," Zeno said, his voice firm, "but considering my history with the SRA, I would have expected a bit more consideration."

Harmony frowned, slowing her pace in the hopes she could glean information before she was spotted. Was she supposed to stay out of sight? Zeno probably would prefer that. But she couldn't, not for this. She just wished she knew what the hell the SRA was.

Someone scoffed and a male voice snapped, "Given your history with us, we would have expected you to know better than to abduct a human girl."

Harmony faltered at the same time as Zeno's low growl rumbled through the room.

"As I told you, I have abducted no one."

The person Harmony had gotten the better glimpse of when she'd made her descent shifted his weight and asked, "Is that why she looks like she's trying to sneak by behind your back, with a giant bruise on her arm? Because she *wasn't* abducted?"

A strange combination of embarrassment, shame, and anger rushed through her all at once, heating her blood and her skin, and Harmony squared her shoulders. She heard Zeno start to speak, but she talked over him. "Maybe I just didn't want to be seen by a couple of judgmental strangers who decided to barge in while I was improperly dressed." She stomped up, her bare feet slapping on the hardwood, until Zeno's hand turned outward as if to stop her from continuing forward. Though she'd never planned to walk past him in the first place. She only wanted line-of-sight for when she gave a piece of her mind to these two and whatever badge they carried. "Are you really accusing Zeno of kidnapping me? Do I *look* kidnapped?"

The leaner of the two, the one Harmony hadn't seen as well, raked a briefly critical gaze over her before staring her straight in the eyes. "You look distressed. Vulnerable. Taking advantage of a young woman like you would be easy for someone like him."

Zeno made a low rumbling sound that felt like a warning. "Harmony is in no danger from me. She can leave at any time of her choosing."

The other male released a tired exhale. "Miss Lace," he said, "if it's true you're free to leave, then help Mr. Darkhan's claim and agree to come with us back to the office."

Harmony felt her brows leap up her forehead. "Excuse me? So, God forbid Zeno take me against my will, but it's perfectly okay for the two of you to blackmail me into going who-the-heck-knows-where? In case you didn't realize, blackmailing someone to come with you is basically kidnapping them."

The leaner male grunted and cut a glare up at Zeno. "If we find out you coached her—"

"Oh for fuck's sake!" Harmony exclaimed, her exasperation bursting from her. "The only thing my parents probably did right was teach me not to just go off with every stranger who asked me to come along with them. Why does that have to be Zeno's fault?"

"I think you're misunderstanding this situation," the tired one said. He raised a hand as if to pacify her. "We aren't attempting to kidnap you, Miss Lace. You've been reported as abducted by a dragon-type shifter matching Zeno Darkhan's description. We need to have a conversation with you, apart from Mr. Darkhan, to get your side of the story."

Harmony folded her arms across her chest. "We can do that here. Zeno has an office he can lend us. He'll sit in another room." It wasn't like she'd asked and she was certain none of the quicker options appealed to him, but of all the ones that felt like compromise, this was the angle she was willing to abide by. For one thing, she was decently covered, not dressed for going out in public.

"For a lot of reasons, that wouldn't work," the same man said, as if explaining a problem to a whining child.

"And you see no problem with attempting to force her to go with you?" Zeno challenged. His tone was hard and even, like steel.

Both unnamed men looked up at him for a beat, and again the leaner one with the attitude spoke first, directing his words back to her. "Tell us about that bruise."

Harmony narrowed her eyes at him. "That's a long and personal story. Tell me who reported me as kidnapped."

"Not here."

"Then maybe you're just full of lies," she snapped. "Zeno said you were some kind of government group, but you haven't even identified yourselves and you're trying to drag me out of here *obviously* against my will. Or what, do you think I'm so fabulous an actress that my attitude is a bluff?"

For the first time, both men looked, if only briefly, taken aback.

In their moment of seeming shock, Zeno said, "You are welcome to use my home, as Harmony has offered, but make no mistake. The moment you lay a finger on her with the intent to force her to your will, I will become hostile." He motioned to the items on the floor, drawing Harmony's attention to them for the first time. "And I expect to receive those back in pristine condition, or a full financial reimbursement. As you can see, Harmony needs clothing. Those are for her."

Her arms fell to her sides as she struggled not to gape. There were two bags, both clearly full, bearing recognizable logos the likes of which she had never imagined touching. The bags were banded shut and had been wrapped together in a thin layer of bubble wrap, making the set appear from a distance like a singular large package. For a moment, as she stared, she felt confused.

Then she remembered the perplexing thing he'd said in the laundry room upstairs and understanding slammed into her, as well as another rush of embarrassment. Harmony dragged in a breath and craned her neck to look up at him. "Did you—"

He met her gaze, and though his lips remained firmly anchored in a frown, his eyes warmed. "Anything I got wrong can be returned or donated. It's just to get you started."

"Started on what?" the leaner man, who stood closest to the bags that apparently were meant for her, said. "The new life you plan to whisk her off to?"

Harmony turned her frown outward once more. "What is the matter with you? Is this what you do, barge into people's homes and bully them into cowing to you? Because trust me, Nameless Fake Government Guy, I have had it up to *here*"—she raised her hand as high as she could reach and still keep her palm flat—"with that antiquated, bullying bullshit." She drew a breath to say more, but the other one spoke up again.

"I do apologize for our oversight, Miss Lace," he said. "This is Agent Ryland, I'm Agent Muller. We're with the SRA."

As he dipped his hand into a pocket, Harmony planted hers on her hips and said pointedly, "What's that, the Scoundrels Ravaging America?"

The one identified as Ryland actually balked, his dark brows arching high on his forehead.

Muller pulled out a wallet-like badge, reminiscent of every FBI ID she'd seen on television, and held it out and open for her inspection. He repeated the words even as her eyes read them, her brain not processing. "The Shifter Relations Agency," he said.

Harmony stared until he pulled the thing she had no way of authenticating away, her mind spinning. "The what?" *Shifter Relations...* She could only think of two ways that could be interpreted, and in one of those ways, she failed to understand their issue with her under Zeno's roof. But the other made even less sense.

Ryland blew out a breath. "It's our job to make sure the shifters don't abuse their strength, in a nutshell. Keep them from turning cities into cage fights, keep them from abducting innocent humans, all that." He mostly glared at Zeno while he spoke.

"Yes," Zeno said, "and I was hoping to have a word soon with your boss about what a fine job you've been doing."

Harmony reached out, feeling suddenly unsteady, and grabbed hold of his arm. He was still shirtless—the hypocrite—so she couldn't latch onto any fabric, just his skin. But it was more than enough to get his attention, though she didn't wait for him to speak before she sought out his gaze. "Is that true? Is that ... what they do?"

His brow furrowed and he inclined his head. "That is what they're supposed to do, yes."

"We are sanctioned by the federal government," Muller said. "Our agency is smaller and less publicly forward than some others, but our authority is no less—"

Harmony spun forward, managing to do so in a way that edged her body closer to Zeno's warmth, and when she spoke over the man, she did so at a shout. "Well, you suck!" Tears burned her eyes and she raised her bruised arm. "For my entire life, my family and everyone else in the whole damn neighborhood—*neighbor-hood*, not street—has been terrorized by some ragtag group of shifters drunk on their own stupid power. My parents pay protection tax and buy groceries for a honey badger that lives three houses down from us. There's a wolf who patrols at night to make sure we all adhere to a curfew. And that honey badger? He's been harassing and molesting me since I hit puberty." She waved her arm almost violently, nearly smacking Muller in the face. "*He* did this, most of it. Yesterday, when my parents decided to dress me up like some hooker and shove me at him. My body was supposed to be a *gift*, and the only way I got out of it was sheer dumb luck. I ran away, and I ran into Zeno. Zeno saved me. You want to round up shifters who hurt people? Start with Patrick fucking Eades."

VOLUME TWO

Chapter Nine

Despite the raw emotion in Harmony's outburst, the men from the SRA hadn't listened. That was the first and last thing Zeno knew before the situation went to shit.

Before his senses and his memory scrambled.

Zeno had a lot of respect for his old friend, but Scott was going to be out two agents when he caught up to them. He had assumed they were from whatever apprehension group dealt with larger-breed shifters, but their hands had been free. Except he'd turned his attention away from the men during Harmony's emotional ranting, his need to protect her and soothe her overriding his need to keep an eye on them. And the choice had cost him.

He'd known a split-second of searing pain, like raw electricity ripping through his blood. The pain was made worse by Harmony's voice screaming his name somewhere beyond his shrinking line of sight. Then it had all gone black.

When Zeno regained consciousness, he was sprawled on the floor in his own penthouse. His body was heavy, lethargic, and the stench of charred flesh lingered in the air.

"Zeno!" Harmony's remembered shriek, something like terror in her usually melodic voice, jolted him fully awake.

Zeno shoved up, his head spinning, and twisted around. He called for her but he knew she wouldn't answer. He knew she wasn't there. The clothes he'd purchased for her while he'd listened to her sob in the shower remained in bags on the floor just feet away.

Anger burned through him. Scott's men had used a fucking specialized taser on him. He hadn't even seen it before it hit him, and since nothing was dangling from his flesh now, he assumed it wasn't one of those projectile types. Or at least, it was something they could easily retrieve. He hadn't exactly gone on missions with the SRA, he hadn't watched them in action. Still, it pissed him off that one of his friend's teams had gone so far as to strike him. It enraged him that they'd laid hands on his mate.

Zeno grabbed the bags, carrying them properly into the penthouse, and dropped them onto the sofa. He fully intended to retrieve her. She would need those later. Then he tugged his phone from his pocket and growled again. The device was fucking dead.

He dragged in a breath, smacked in the face with Harmony's scent, mixed with the less prominent smells of the two men who'd ultimately taken her away, and the breakfast they'd shared earlier. The aroma of her long-faded arousal when he'd eaten her out on the kitchen island. The stench of his own burned flesh. That still hurt like a bastard, too.

Zeno ripped off his sweatpants, throwing them aside as he strode for the balcony.

It was too much. They'd pushed too far.

There was a reason it was ill-advised to fuck with dragons.

He would kill Patrick Eades for everything the bastard had ever done to Harmony. Then he would go to the SRA's headquarters and take back his mate. As a matter of fact, if he could find them, he'd pick up Larry and Linda Lace along the way and bring them with him. They wanted to accuse him of plucking people up out of the sky, perhaps he should show them what that *really* looked like.

The shift came over him hot and fast, a reflection of his mood. His wings stretched out as soon as they were formed, pulling his weight from the balcony before it became too much for the structure to bear. By the time he was above the building, the shift was settled. His flesh was gone in favor of thicker, armor-like scales. His body size had increased, his arms and legs thickening, claws sprouting where stubby nails had been. His tail swished freely, violently, through the air as he immediately propelled himself forward, aimed directly at Harmony's old neighborhood. He let out a steady, almost hissing exhale, releasing a cloud of smoke to help disguise himself from anyone below as he moved.

He didn't generally like risking daytime flights in populated cities, even if the smoke cloud technique worked nine times out of ten.

This wasn't a normal situation. This time, he didn't give a fuck. Let some human see him. Let some human post it on YouTube. They'd probably get rich or get ridiculed, it made no difference to him.

Harmony's neighborhood came into view less than a minute later and Zeno's focus sharpened. He'd failed her already once that day. He couldn't show his face before her again until he had something to offer her as penance. He would not fail her again.

He spotted her family's house from the air and ground his teeth against the urge to set it ablaze. It was Harmony's right to decide the fate of her parents. He would do no more than frighten them. Bruise them, perhaps. He dragged his gaze away, remembering how she had previously described the setup of her street. Eades's residence was across the street, and only a scant three rooftops away.

Zeno dropped to the ground as he shifted back into a form that would allow him to communicate, landing on his knees just feet from the postage-stamp porch. It was late morning on a weekday, this was a working-class neighborhood. None of that meant no one would notice a monster falling from the sky, or a naked man in the yard.

That was fine. Eades was a coward who liked the spotlight. A humiliating death in front of everyone he'd bullied for years would be fitting.

Zeno stomped up onto the porch, letting his weight carry through and break the old wood beneath his feet even as he took hold of the door and ripped it from its hinges. He let the broken door fall to the side and continued into the dark, unkempt dwelling.

He wasn't an expert on ordinary honey badgers, but surely they lived in better conditions than this. Perhaps Eades was actually a rat.

Patrick Eades came barreling around the far corner, tugging up his pants as he walked and already shouting. "What the fu—" His eyes blew wide and his face drained of color. The pants slipped from his fingers, hanging unbuttoned from his hips. "You."

"Yes," Zeno said, letting more smoke curl from his mouth as he spoke. "*Me.*" He continued forward, stepping around a love seat that was well past its prime without ever taking his eyes from his target.

Eades slid one foot backward and swallowed hard. "You can't just—you destroyed my fucking door, asshole!"

Zeno didn't break stride. "You will never again threaten my mate, or any other woman."

Eades's lips curled, his shoulders tightening. For a moment, he only glared as Zeno closed the distance between them, until finally he let out an enraged roar and threw himself forward. His body rippled as his own shift overtook him, the denim falling to the floor as a smaller body covered in black and silver fur propelled through the air. The momentum he'd given himself almost guaranteed he would make first contact, his own claws extended.

Were Zeno human, the attack would rip open his abdomen.

Zeno caught the flying sack of fur-covered-shit by its throat, mindless of the creature's tinier claws, and pivoted around to slam the beast into the nearest wall. The drywall cracked, caving in from the impact.

Eades made a sound of pain, going limp for a second before exploding into a wild, wiggling frenzy. He scratched and kicked, continuously trying to twist his head around in order to bite, but none of it made a difference. There was absolutely nothing about Patrick Eades that posed a threat.

Zeno growled low and a lick of flame slipped from his lips, heating the air between them. "Never again." His arm shifted in the span of seconds. By necessity he lost his advantageous grip on the honey badger's throat, but before the smaller beast could scamper away, he swept downward with his own claws.

Blood sprayed the walls and dripped onto the floor. Zeno felt some of it splatter his own skin.

Eades made a weak, strained sound and finally shifted back into his human form. "F-fuck, stop … please, stop."

Zeno scowled. "Please?" He made a show of stretching and flexing his claws. "Would you have listened to Harmony if she begged you to stop? If she said *please*?"

Eades's breathing was shallow, blood still trickling from the wound that hadn't fully closed with his shift. He couldn't look away from Zeno's claws. "I-I…"

"I didn't think so." Zeno plunged his claws into

Eades's chest, curled them around the fucker's heart, and squeezed until it gave. Then he lifted the bleeding corpse, followed his protesting nose to the restroom, and dropped the body into the tub. It was easy enough to toss the flimsy shower curtain aside, and with a single exhale, he lit Patrick Eades's body ablaze.

From beyond the restroom, he heard someone shout for the newly deceased honey badger. Over the death and blood it was hard to catch the newcomer's scent, but Zeno had a decent guess. He turned away from the burning body, right arm still shifted and covered in blood, and strode down the hall as heavy footfalls came in his direction.

A man—a wolf—came to an abrupt stop at the sight of him. His eyes darted to Zeno's bloodied arm and he let out a growl. "Who the fuck are you? Where's Ricky?"

"You must be the wolf Harmony spoke of," Zeno replied. "Eades is in the tub, burning." The wolf's eyes went wide for a moment before darkening with rage. "I didn't come for you, but if you think you're going to pose a problem for me or my mate, I will do the same to you regardless." At the end of his declaration, Zeno allowed another lick of flame to slide from his lips.

He knew how it looked. He still remembered, even three hundred years since the last time he'd seen it, when his father had used the same intimidation tactic. It was a tactic that had scared even his allies.

The wolf before him, too young and inexperienced to have ever endured that sort of cruelty, was no exception. The fight left his eyes in an instant and he flinched back, making space for Zeno to pass. "Y-you're the dragon ... fuck." His gaze darted down the hall. Smoke had begun drifting from the room, and no doubt the canine shifter could smell what was underneath. "Fuck."

Zeno continued forward. "Wise choice." He gave his arm a good shake, knowing the blood would fall from his scales with his shift, and continued to the door. He had one more stop to make and no desire to linger.

VOLUME TWO

Chapter Ten

Harmony wasn't sure how long she'd been left alone in the unremarkable room once Agents Jack and Ass had finally left, but it felt like eternity. Neither prick had wanted to accept that she wasn't being somehow brainwashed or intimidated into putting on an act in front of Zeno. They'd insisted she was *safe* in the new space, safe to speak openly and honestly, so she'd firmly told them they were the real kidnappers and she wanted to be taken back. That wasn't what they'd wanted to hear, apparently. So they'd declared that she needed "a moment to breathe" and left her to herself, in a locked room she was somehow not supposed to see as a cage.

Left alone, Harmony had plenty of time to reflect and take stock. Her foot throbbed in a perfect example of terrible irony, an underscore to everything that had gone wrong that morning. She hadn't even made it through the parking garage barefoot—granted, she'd been struggling her best—without stepping on something hurting her foot. For which she had been handed a wad of tissues to hold over the wound while she was driven away.

Her first thought when she'd finally processed the pain was that Zeno would be so mad. He'd gone to such trouble to protect her feet, and she'd left her new boots in the bedroom.

Her second thought was no coherent thought at all. Just a vivid, breath-stealing memory of the moment she'd watched Zeno's back arch and his eyes roll back in his head. The moment she'd seen him drop to the ground with barely a sound. He'd been facing her. He'd been distracted by her. Neither of them had seen whatever had hit him coming, and it was her fault. Her fault he'd been hurt. Her fault he'd been left unconscious, unsupervised, on the floor of his own home.

Her throat threatened to close just thinking about it. She was no fighter. She'd done her best to resist when Jack and Ass had grabbed hold of her, declaring she was coming with them for "her own good," but it hadn't made a difference. She might have bruised one. They'd bruised her worse. Not that she cared. She was much more worried about Zeno, who could still for all she knew be lying on his own floor and struggling to breathe. Or not breathing at all.

If she made it out of this alive, she was finding a lawyer and suing the ever-loving crap out of this so-called government agency. Even if she spent the rest of her life paying that lawyer off.

The door at the far side of the room finally swung open, startling her into focus, and Harmony jerked back too forcefully. Her still-sore foot dragged across the cold, hard surface of the floor. She hoped the unfamiliar, older male stepping into the room mistook her sharp gasp as anything other than a sign of pain. Pain was weakness to assholes like them.

He didn't say a word as he pushed the door shut, never taking his eyes from her. He looked her over as if studying her, his expression impassive, and only when he was done did he move forward to pull out the chair across from her. He stayed silent as he settled his sturdy, but not overly broad frame into the seat. So, Harmony took the opportunity to study him, too. The man looked to be at least in his fifties, had a hard face and hair that was as gray as it was brown. He was either already displeased or had a mean disposition, and with that being all she could read about him, her nerves only spiked higher.

But mean or not, she had to hold out. She had to make it through whatever the hell this was. So she curled her arms around herself as best she could, letting her old bruise show and doing her best to make sure the new, still tender scrape on her opposite arm also showed. She didn't think that one had bled, but it had hurt almost enough to distract from her foot.

"You made quite a scene, Miss Lace." He definitely sounded displeased. And there was something distantly familiar in his voice.

Harmony gave him her best glare. "Most people do when they're being kidnapped."

His brow twitched. "You're not kidnapped."

"Really? Then why the heck was I locked in here? Why was I dragged out of the place I wanted to be?" She pulled her arm forward to point at the scrape she herself could only half see. "Why were they so rough with me I have literal scrapes and bruises, and a freaking hole in my foot that no one's bothered to even ask about since I got here?"

His gaze lingered on the scrape. "I will talk to them about the way they handled you," he said, as if he were capitulating with a child, "but you were brought here—"

She smacked her palms on the table. "Against. My. Will." She'd have stood up if her foot didn't hurt and her heart wasn't racing so fast she was worried the movement would make her faint. "And conveniently, now I'm indecently dressed, lacking shoes, and too injured and ill-equipped to walk back to where I *want* to be. None of which gives you the right to keep me."

His scowl somehow deepened. "Are you done? I'm too busy for a spoiled brat throwing a temper tantrum. So if you don't want to be here, delaying this conversation won't help."

Rage licked through her and this time Harmony did push to her feet. "Your people hurt my dragon!" She screamed the words without even meaning to, the truth and fear tearing from her. "I have every right to be *hysterical* right now, you ass! I'm bleeding and bruised and vulnerable, and if my mate knew about this he would burn your whole building to the ground!" She sucked in a breath, unable to stop the tears even as her voice lowered and began to shake. "But you don't care about that. You don't care about any of the things you claim to. So, what, are you going to ship me off to be raped and beaten?" She dropped back into her seat, suddenly weak. "Or are you just here to kill me?"

She hadn't realized, in her blinding tirade, that the man's mask had finally cracked. She didn't realize it until he reached up and pinched the bridge of his nose in clear exasperation. "Your mate." He pushed out a sigh as if he were overburdened. "Goddammit, Darkhan, just be straight for once," he said quieter, as if muttering to himself.

Harmony blinked.

The man straightened, arm lowering, and aimed his frown again at her. "He told you you're his mate?"

"Yes." She swallowed a lump of emotion in her throat. "And your people left him for dead."

"He was stunned, not decapitated," the man said with a low grunt. "He's probably already awake by now." He sighed again. "Though that means the other part of what you said would be true. Fuck." He braced his hands on the table as if he were going to stand but didn't move, and after another moment, let his arms fall. "Harmony, I'm going to ask you something that will upset you. For the sake of conversation, pretend I'm ignorant and this is your golden opportunity."

She frowned but slowly inclined her head. It wasn't like she had a lot of options.

The man leaned forward and folded his arms on

the table. "Muller and Ryland told me what you said about the neighborhood where your family lives. I need to know if you were exaggerating or fabricating any portion of that story."

Harmony bit her lips as the urge to yell at him rose in her chest again. Yelling wasn't getting her anywhere anyway, and she didn't generally enjoy it. She'd just never been so angry. So distressed. It needed to come out. But she pushed the feeling down as best she could and finally said, "I oversimplified. But you don't really strike me as the caring stranger type, and frankly, I haven't been given any reason to tear open my own psychological wounds. Besides, it's not like that Shifter Relations thing is anything more than a scare tactic for the well-behaved ones like Zeno, right?"

It was the last thing she said that seemed to reach him. The man who hadn't introduced himself frowned, again, but this frown was deeper. Darker. There was something angry in it that Harmony couldn't place. Something that felt genuine. "No," he said, "it's supposed to be exactly the opposite." This time he did shove to his feet, the chair scraping behind him. "I knew something was sideways when I heard the report, but Muller and Ryland were already en route. That isn't justification for letting it get this far. You have my—"

Muffled shouting interrupted him, drawing both their attention to the door seconds before it crashed open so hard it stuck in the wall. The shouting continued, but Harmony only heard it for another second.

Her heart jump-started in her chest as she drank in the ludicrous but entirely welcomed sight of her dragon lover standing just inside the doorway. Nude. Furious. And holding both her parents like sacks of potatoes under his arms.

A stupid smile split her face and tears of relief

burned her eyes before she'd even found her voice.

"Darkhan, what the hell are you doing?" the other man in the room demanded, sounding more shocked than angry.

Zeno turned a hard glare on the man and unceremoniously deposited Harmony's unconscious mother onto the table. There were no obvious wounds on her, though her hair was a wild mess, but she was obviously out. He promptly swung her groaning father around and dropped him to the floor at the government man's feet. "*Now* I am guilty of plucking humans off the ground and absconding with them." His nostrils flared and his chest expanded with a deep breath.

Harmony shook as she finally pushed to her feet. "Zeno…" She couldn't even see a burn mark on his skin. Was it stupid that she'd looked for one?

The image of him crumbling to the floor flashed once again through her mind and she decided it wasn't. Just as she knew she didn't care about the discomfort in her foot or their audience when she all but threw herself forward. "Zeno!"

Her foot never made another moment of contact with the floor. In a heartbeat, Harmony found herself swept up in Zeno's strong embrace, one of his hands threaded through her hair at the back of her head, and the other arm tucked beneath her butt for support. He held her tight, his head bent so he could drag his nose beside her ear and down the line of her neck. And she realized she didn't even know what to say first. So, she curled her arms around his shoulders and let herself breathe him in.

"Forgive me, Little Dove," Zeno murmured against her skin. "If I had acted sooner, you wouldn't be hurting now. I am sorry."

Harmony pushed down her overemotional tears and bumped her head lightly into his in lieu of pulling away. "I've been so worried about you…"

Distinct throat-clearing suddenly reminded her they weren't alone, or really in a place to be having a personal conversation. No matter how comfortable she felt in Zeno's arms.

Zeno adjusted his stance, not relaxing his grip or setting her down. "Your men caused injury to my mate," he said in a low, dangerous tone, "and you left her to sit here and bleed. I thought better of you than that, Scott."

Scott? Harmony's eyes widened as understanding dawned. The man she'd been speaking to, sort of, when Zeno had burst in was the man who'd called minutes before their day had gone sideways?

She couldn't see him anymore, but she recognized the sound of Scott's sigh. "I had been told the wound was superficial. Unlike you, I don't have super-senses, I had no way to know she was still bleeding." His tone shifted as he spoke. "I recognize that's an issue, Darkhan, but it could have been avoided if you'd just told someone who she is to you. What am I supposed to do with this?" Harmony couldn't see him, but she pictured the grumpy-faced man gesturing to her almost-silent parents as his words sharpened.

"Arrest them," Zeno said. "Fine them. Fucking chase them out of the city with pitchforks for all I care. They're the ones who reported Harmony as abducted and we both know it—just as we both know she *wasn't*. I believe filing false reports is a crime in your legal system."

"You want them punished my way?" Scott's question was cautious.

Zeno's thumb rubbed almost absently over Harmony's scalp. "They are my mate's blood. I would prefer not to kill them with my own hand."

Harmony felt her throat constrict and twisted her

hands in the back of Zeno's hair. She had a lot of issues with her parents. At this point, she questioned whether she even truly loved them. She certainly didn't trust them. But wanting them dead? No. That would only make the loss and damage of her childhood worse if she ended up being the reason they died.

Her father made a sound like he might finally be regaining his senses.

Something metallic clinked faintly in the air. "There's still the matter of that gang she mentioned," Scott said. The metallic sound happened again, in conjunction with the rustling of fabric, as it clicked and rattled.

Harmony's father immediately shouted in protest. "Hey! What—"

"I'll get to you in a minute, Mr. Lace," Scott said. There was some more rustling, something like shuffled steps, and the sound of a body settling heavily into a chair.

"You can't—Linda! What the hell is going on?" The briefest of pauses. "Harmony?"

Harmony pressed her forehead into the crook of Zeno's neck. She'd never heard her usually almost passive father so riled, and it gave her no sense of peace or justice. The entire situation just made her want to be sick.

Zeno's hand lowered to her nape and he said, "My vendetta with that gang is settled. Yours, I believe, has only just begun. If you find yourself in need of information from Harmony, I expect you to call ahead and ask politely."

Her father called for her mother again, the metallic sound clinking in time to another rustling of fabric. He didn't seem able to focus long enough to follow the scene from his perspective.

Scott spoke up again. "If she has anything to say to them, now would be the best time."

Zeno gave her neck a gentle squeeze.

Harmony swallowed. "This is their fault," she whispered, her words feeling too raw. She thought to say she had no words left for them, but before she could, something new occurred to her. So, she drew a breath and lifted her head, forcing herself to turn it enough to see a portion of the room.

She saw her mother, still slumped unconscious on the table, legs dangling off the side. And she saw her father, awake and wide-eyed but somehow not looking overly alert, sitting in the chair Scott had previously occupied. Her father's arms were behind his back in a way he never sat normally, pitching his body slightly forward … as if he were handcuffed.

Harmony settled her gaze on her father, for what good it would do. "I've decided to make my own choices from now on."

Her father's mouth opened. "But—"

"Goodbye." She turned her head away, not giving him the satisfaction of seeing the tear that slipped down her cheek anyway.

Zeno pressed her head gently back into the groove of his throat. "You and I will talk another time," he said, she assumed to Scott.

Scott made a sound like a pained sigh. "Nothing about you leaving the way you came in is good for any of us. Let me have someone drive you, or wait in another room until Roland can get here."

This time it was Zeno who made a displeased sound.

Harmony's mouth opened before she could stop herself, though she at least kept her voice soft. "You're naked." He seemed to go still and her runaway mouth continued. "Like, all-the-way naked, you hypocrite."

The hand locked around her thigh gave a squeeze. "A ride home, then. From a driver not attracted to the male form. My Little Dove has decided not to share."

"Oh, for fuck's sake." Something like stomping preceded Scott's voice shouting away from them. "I need someone with muscle, a first-aid kit, and a goddamn sheet!"

Harmony tried to squirm, at least enough to see the room, but Zeno lowered a hand to her shoulders and held her in place.

"Patience, Little Dove."

All she could do was push out a breath, listen to the increased sounds of movement, and wait. At least, with Zeno's arms around her, she felt safe. Even her new pains were a faded memory against his warmth. Best of all, she could hear his steady heartbeat beneath her ear. She could feel his strength in his hold. He was alive and well.

She knew now how much the idea of him being anything else distressed her. She didn't know how she would have handled never seeing him again. Probably that meant he was right about the whole destiny thing.

Chapter Eleven

"Let me see your foot, Little Dove," Zeno said, his voice full of all the things Harmony felt as though she was lacking at the moment—gentleness and patience, primarily.

"My foot's totally fine," Harmony said. She obediently bent down and unfastened her cute shoes enough to slip her feet free anyway. "I haven't even limped in days." He was way too overprotective. He hadn't let her put any weight whatsoever on her foot for three whole days, and even a week after she'd insisted on doing her own walking again, he never went far.

Zeno planted his hands on her hips and hefted her onto the countertop. "I was away for most of today, and rumor has it you finally went shopping. Indulge me."

She pretended to pout. "Roland's such a tattletale." Not that she'd thought for a second he would do anything different. "It was only a couple of stores. I felt a little ill looking at those price tags. I don't think I'm used to that part yet."

Zeno chuckled and swept his hands down her leg, cupping her calf as his fingertips teased up the top of her foot. "Yet, hm?" He crouched down, adjusting his grip as he moved.

"What are you even looking for? It can't still be visible."

He gently ran his thumb over the pad of her foot. "Signs of infection. You didn't get proper initial treatment." He gave her foot a squeeze, lowered her leg, and stood. "You were lucky."

Harmony smiled. He'd been so worried about her foot and her mental state after everything that she'd felt a little awkward trying to tell him what she'd realized that day in the SRA office. He had probably been right that she needed at least a short amount of time to process the damage. But in a lot of ways, her relationship with her family had been strained at best, so losing it completely wasn't hard to adjust to. And she was tired of waiting. "Is it better now?"

"It looks much better, yes," Zeno said, leaning toward her for a kiss.

She leaned up to meet his lips with hers, just a passing brush, and hopped from the counter before he could pin her in place again. She did love the way he took control, the way he touched her and kissed her, but she wanted to tease him just a tiny bit. So she took advantage of his surprise, slipped past him, and darted for the glass partition that led to the balcony.

As always, it was windy out, making the otherwise sturdy structure suddenly feel a little less secure. Her hair whipped immediately across her face and the knee-length skirt of her overpriced dress tangled around her legs.

"Are we playing tag, Little Dove?" Zeno asked, having followed her to stand at the doorway.

Harmony turned to face him, smiling wide. "No. We're playing catch." She put her back to the rail and reached behind her, curling her fingers around the cool metal.

"Harmony," Zeno said cautiously, his amber eyes narrowing. He took a step forward.

"The game is simple," she said, her smile unwavering. She carefully pulled herself up only so that she was perched on the edge, her grip strong despite the relentless tug of the wind. "You have something I want, I have something you want. So, you will catch me, and in doing so, we'll both get our something."

He didn't look at all reassured. "I would give you anything—"

"Yes. Yet in nearly two weeks, I haven't once seen the other side of you. How can I possibly tie myself to you for the rest of my life if I don't even know what you look like half the time?" She let her words linger, waited until his eyes widened with the beginnings of understanding. "Catch," she said, and threw herself over.

Trust falls were hard. But she doubted anyone at any concert or rave had anything on her and her trust fall from thirty-whatever stories up. Certain death awaited her if she had miscalculated or if her dragon hesitated too long. She knew all of that before she'd put the plan into motion, just as she'd made sure nothing stupid was in her way, like a lower-level balcony or any sort of pole-like protrusion.

There really hadn't been any planning ahead for the way the wind ripped by too fast and too hard to even breathe, let alone scream. It was intense. Terrifying. For a long second, her gut twisted with the fear that she'd made a mistake.

Her eyes shifted to the side with a blur of dark movement in her descending peripheral vision even as a rush of contradictory heat surrounded her. Something like a cushion of air pushed up at her from below, slowing her gravity-induced plummet, and the next thing she knew she had landed on a solid surface. A solid, almost slick, surface of dark blue accentuated with the deepest black wings and a thick mane of matching ebony just above her. A surface that moved.

Harmony gasped for breath and scrambled to grab hold of the mane, rolling her body enough to straddle the ridge of spine between the wings as she did so. No sooner was she settled, her eyes wide at the cityscape view now beneath her that she hadn't really thought to imagine, than her fantastical steed veered to the side.

She cried out in surprise but kept hold, tears from the bite of the wind pricking her eyes. Laughter was pulling up from her belly by the time they were lowering again.

Then, with a start, the hair beneath her fingers receded and her dragon practically vanished in favor of a gloriously naked man. They dropped as he twisted in the air, catching her in his arms as he landed squarely on their previously departed balcony.

Harmony drew a deep breath. "That was—"

Zeno pinned her to the glass in a rush of movement, lifting her arms over her head. "Are you trying to kill yourself?"

Right. She had guessed he would probably be upset with her choice of tactic.

Harmony offered him a calm smile. "No." She stretched her fingers and curled them over his hands as best she could. "I want you, Zeno. I want *us*. And I wanted to make it clear that I want all of you, not just the human side you usually wear around me." She licked her wind-chapped lips. "I was hoping to show you—to prove to you—that I trust you. I trust you completely."

His burning stare dropped down her frame for a lingering second and his Adam's apple bobbed with a hard swallow. "Harmony," he said, his voice rough. "You don't have to do reckless things for that."

"I know. But every once in a while, something a little reckless might be fun…" She trailed off and used his own strength to hook her legs over his hips, drawing their bodies closer. "Will you let me see more of you, if I ask without jumping from high places?"

Zeno groaned low and bowed his head, dragging his nose the length of her throat. "I'll take you somewhere it's safer for me to linger in that form and let you gaze to your heart's content, if that's what you want." He moved her hands into one of his, then reached down and lowered the zipper of her dress. "More importantly, Little Dove, are you sure you want this? I need to hear the words."

Harmony crossed her ankles over his butt, rocking her clothed center against his freshly risen erection, and sought out his almost glowing eyes. "Am I sure I want you to fuck me so hard I can't walk again? Or am I sure I want to accept you forever and do that soul-bonding thing you talked about? Because the answer is yes, Zeno Darkhan. I am very sure." She watched his eyes widen a little, felt his chest heave with a hard breath, and softened her tone as much as she dared. "I love you, Zeno."

Zeno growled and crushed his lips to hers, releasing her hands in favor of peeling the loosened dress down enough to let her boobs spill free. His tongue pushed into her mouth and he moved one hand to palm a breast while the other dipped lower to reach below and squeeze her ass.

Harmony mewled against him, shoving her fingers into his loose hair and arching into his touch. He kissed her fiercely, his thumb rolling over her nipple as he rocked his length over her. Then all at once he broke the kiss, trailing his lips and tongue across her jaw, and the hand at her chest lowered to join the other beneath her skirt.

"Tell me now while I can think," he said, his fingers dipping beneath her panties, "where do you want my mark, Little Dove?"

She gasped as he pumped two fingers into her aching core and curled them inside her. "I-I only get one?"

She felt him smirk against her before promptly sucking a hickey into her skin. "Only one that's *permanent*."

Harmony did her best to think through her options. She always loved when Zeno teased her with his teeth, it never mattered where. She also loved when he buried his face in her neck or her hair, or the valley between her boobs. To say nothing for between her legs, of course.

"Harmony," Zeno said, voice thick and husky. "I need an answer."

She sucked in a breath, realizing her brain was becoming muddled. "M-my neck," she said, panting. "Where you like to nuzzle me."

His chest vibrated with a low hum of approval. "Good girl." He extended his thumb and rolled it across her clit, and just like that she shuddered in blistering release. Harmony was still gasping for breath when he ripped her panties from her, but instead of letting the shredded material blow away, he turned his head and puffed out a small flame. Incinerating them.

She choked on a laugh. "Did you—really?"

Zeno pushed her skirt up to her waist and leaned in to trail more kisses along her jaw. "You thought I'd let your used panties be found by someone else?"

Harmony rolled her eyes, still laughing, and tugged on his hair until he raised his head for a wet kiss. She felt him pushing at her entrance and rocked her hips in invitation.

Zeno broke the kiss with a possessive growl. "Now, and forever, you are *mine*." He dipped his head, and she nearly missed the blurry ripple of skin that indicated a partial shift before his face was out of sight. An instant later he snapped his hips forward, filling her in a single satisfying thrust that had her crying out. Something briefly sharp and intensely warm shot through her at her neck even as she adjusted to his girth, sending searing, almost overwhelming pleasure coursing through her.

Harmony clung to him as her body rode the wave, feeling cognizant and yet not at the same time. She knew only that she was in Zeno's arms, and she'd never felt so good.

Zeno rocked with her for a moment before dragging out and slamming back into her pussy, his fingers digging into her ass to hold her hips mostly still. She felt his tongue slide up her neck, then down to dip between her breasts, before retreating from her skin. His hips never stopped. Once he started thrusting he became like a man possessed, driving his thick length in and out of her body in deep strokes.

The next orgasm crashed over her without warning and Harmony screamed her ecstasy, his name disappearing into the wind still whipping around them.

Zeno stepped away from the window, turned, and lowered Harmony to her feet. He bent her forward and moved her hands to the railing, purposefully curling her fingers around the metal bars before kicking her feet wide.

The breath rushed from her as she realized his intent, fresh excitement coursing through her. She had her dress on, but her boobs were dangling free and her panties were nonexistent, so the dress was a strange technicality. Although the nearest neighboring skyscraper didn't actually have a facing view.

Then her brain shut off as Zeno slid his cock over her sopping, exposed pussy before driving himself inside once more. He held her hips in a bruising grip and grunted a curse she barely heard over the wind. "*Fuck*, Harmony, you fit me so well. I'm going to fill you up every day until your belly is swollen with our child."

She had to lower her forehead to the cool metal

railing. "Yes, yes, please," she said on a gasp. She pushed her hips backward as best she could, trying to grind against him. "Zeno!"

He slammed into her one more time and let out a roar, a larger burst of flame filling the air—warming the air—overhead as he finally released inside her.

Harmony followed him over, another shout tearing from her lips.

Their hips rocked together for several long seconds before her knees threatened to buckle. He caught her around the waist, sweeping her up into his arms, and she offered him a tired laugh. "I think I'm ready to go inside now."

Zeno bent down and kissed her gently. "Then that's what we'll do, my dove."

Harmony let her eyes close as he carried her inside, her head resting on his broad shoulder. The chill from the relentless wind disappeared as soon as they crossed the threshold, though she'd long since stopped paying it any real attention.

Zeno carried her up the stairs, all the way to the bedroom they'd been sharing since the first night he'd brought her to the penthouse, and sat her on the bed. Only then did he peel off her dress. He dropped to his knees and peppered kisses up her legs, his always-trimmed beard occasionally scratching against her skin as he tilted his head for a new angle. His hands kneaded her flesh, squeezing and rubbing as he slowly climbed higher. He deftly avoided her center as he ascended her body, his touch and his kisses prompting her to lie back on the bed.

By the time he swept his tongue over the first nipple, she was breathless again. "Z-Zeno…"

He didn't linger there, gliding across her skin to deliver the same attention to her other breast before continuing up. He took hold of her arms and stretched them over her head, his tongue lingered over the new mark she hadn't yet seen at the base of her neck, and she swore her blood caught fire. Then he resumed his path up, nibbled on her earlobe, and finally dropped a light kiss to her nose.

Harmony sucked in a breath. "What…?"

He smiled, his eyes warm with a strange but endearing mix of affection and desire. "Am I not allowed to appreciate my mate's beauty?"

A strangled laugh escaped her. He'd just had his hands and his lips over nearly every inch of her. There was no hiding her rolls from him. Yet he still managed to say that as if it were an undeniable fact. "You are." It was a weak response, but her brain was mush.

Zeno leaned down and kissed her properly, pressing his lips to hers before slowly working his tongue into her mouth. The kiss was wet and thorough and despite the hunger she sensed in him, he took his time with her. He never released her hands. When the kiss finally broke, both breathing heavily, he said, "You understand I do not merely want you as my mate, Harmony."

She blinked at him. "You want to knock me up that bad?"

A devilish smirk lifted his lips. "In fact I do." He let go of her hands in favor of reaching down to anchor onto her hips and proceeded to rock his pelvis against hers, gliding his renewed erection over her pussy. "Every inch of you, inside and out, will only ever be mine. But to some extent, I will share that claim with our children." He pushed himself inside her as he spoke, moving slowly enough that her eyes rolled back in her head and her back arched before he was settled.

Harmony panted, her vision bleary but her heart racing. She stretched out a hand, reaching for him.

Zeno lowered himself over her again, rocking slow, driving himself deep in a mostly grinding motion as he crushed her torso up to his. He kissed her, rough and wet, then trailed yet more kisses down her throat on the side he hadn't yet marked.

Harmony curled her arms around him as best she could, her fingers digging into his skin. "I-I'm already yours," she said, gasping as she fought for words. "All of me. You have me. You'll always have me."

He growled low, nipped at her skin, and pushed up to his elbows to find her gaze again. "And the world will know, regardless of their species. We are mated, and soon you will be my wife."

What little breath she had rushed from her lungs as his declaration echoed like a church bell in her head. *Wife.* The wife of Zeno Darkhan.

Harmony moved her hands to grab hold of his face and pull him down for a fierce kiss, causing his rhythm to falter. The harder snap of his hips had her breaking away to choke on a scream and she twisted her fingers in his hair. "Yes! Please, yes!"

Zeno moved his lips to her ear. "Fly with me, then, my dove." He thrust into her again and ground down, their bodies already tilted at the perfect angle for the motion to add friction to her clit.

She felt him release in a hot burst, deep inside her, and her body chased after him into oblivion. Harmony clung to his shoulders as she shook, tears rolling from her eyes with the intensity of the orgasm and emotion he'd roused in her. It felt so good it almost hurt and she didn't want it to end. She didn't ever want it to end.

Zeno wedged his arms beneath her after several seconds, his own breathing ragged, and hauled her up without dislodging her. "I love you, too, Harmony," he murmured into her hair. "And I swear to you, no matter how the world changes, you will have me. Always."

She sucked in a breath, managed to curl her arms more thoroughly around his shoulders, and closed her eyes as he started them toward the bathroom. "Always," she whispered back. "I'll always be your Little Dove."

VOLUME TWO

Epilogue

Three Years Later

"Settling your tab?" The old bartender raised a silver brow even as he rested his fingertips over the top of Zeno's card. "You're a creature of habit, old friend. The last time you cleared your tab you were newly mated."

Zeno chuckled, tipping the glass still in his hand in acknowledgment before knocking back what remained of the drink. One wouldn't hurt, and for old-time's sake, it felt right. "Don't look so worried, Clive. I'm just going away for a while. It would be rude of me to leave a balance hanging, no matter how well I know the owners are doing."

Clive hummed and swept the card through the requisite machine. "I heard you've pulled from the last of your local business affiliations. Is everything all right with the family?" He handed back the card as he spoke.

Zeno slid the glass forward and accepted the piece of plastic that passed for money, tucking it back into his wallet. "Of course. You think I'd be worried about a small bar tab if there was something wrong with Harmony, or Nova?" Even the theoretical thought made his insides twist as though his organs were caught in a clawed vice. He pushed it down and offered the man across from him a genuine smile. Every word he said here would get back to Dario, so it saved him the trouble of one more phone call. "Now that Nova's a little older, Harmony wants to see some of the places I've told her about. We were only able to travel the one time before our daughter was born, I think she's feeling restless."

Clive's lips twitched. "I wouldn't expect a dragon's mate to be overly complacent in one place for long." He lifted the glass. "I'm glad to hear you're heading out for good reasons for once."

Zeno grunted, unable to deny the accusation, bade the bartender a temporary farewell, and made one more exit from The Gin Room. Roland was already waiting for him and the car was in motion as soon as Zeno clicked his seat belt into place. Flying would have been faster, but he generally tried to play by the rules while he was living among society.

"Will you be away for a while, sir?" Roland asked as they neared the building.

"Yes," Zeno said. "We're going to let the penthouse go, but Harmony wants to come back to New York eventually. I'll need you to be my eyes for that when the time comes, so don't worry about your income. Just enjoy the respite."

Roland's response was hesitant, the scent of surprise wafting from him. "Sir ... thank you."

As the car rolled to a stop in the parking garage, Zeno released the restrictive belt and said, "Loyalty is always rewarded, Roland. You've been good to me. Now, get some rest, our flight leaves early tomorrow and we'll need one more drive."

"I'll bring coffee and cocoa."

Zeno clapped his long-time employee—currently his only employee—on the shoulder, climbed from the car, and strode swiftly to the elevator. He supposed he was glad he hadn't paid some black-market agency to remove the box in favor of being able to fly himself up and down, in hindsight. Though he remembered he'd been tempted once. Whatever home they chose when they returned to the New York area, it would need to have land for their children, and most importantly, not be restricted by technological boxes.

He could hear the giggling before he was even

through the inner door, and any irritation faded away.

"Daddy's going to love it," Harmony was saying as he stepped through the door. Her sweet voice was laced with laughter and adoration.

Young giggling from the same direction assured him she was standing with their two-year-old, and both females were facing the wall of windows he'd had to have enhanced security put in to keep their toddler from climbing through. And then he saw what they were looking at. Little Nova had taken her new children's paint set and decorated the glass.

Zeno smiled as he approached. "I see we have new artwork."

Harmony turned a bright smile up to him, her blue eyes shining. They'd gained so much more life and vibrancy since she'd separated from her parents. Even her skin, still naturally pale, had a permanently healthier glow. And as it always did, the sight of her standing in front of him made him want to haul her closer, to leave more marks on that beautiful skin and watch the way those eyes sparkled when she climaxed. To feel her tremble in release in his arms. She was a hard woman to resist, his mate.

"Daddy!" Nova launched herself at his legs, latching on with all her little might—which was still entirely manageable at her young age. "Do you like it?" She tipped her head back and blinked blue eyes that perfectly matched her mother's up at him, grinning wide beneath her head of wild, dark hair she'd inherited from him.

Zeno smiled and scooped her up, setting her on his shoulder. She was his daughter, after all, and when she hit puberty she would start shifting. She already loved high places. "I do," he said, obediently studying the scribbled mess painted onto the window again. "It's a masterpiece."

Harmony laughed and stepped up to him, reaching up to teasingly tickle Nova's bare foot. "I think we should leave it for the next owner."

"Agreed." He met her gaze. "However, Wife, is there something else?"

"Yes." She pushed up on her tiptoes and stretched her arms around his torso, her voice softening. "Welcome home."

"Kiss, kiss, kiss!" Nova squealed, squirming on his shoulder even as he leaned forward to do exactly that.

Zeno lingered on Harmony's lips for a long second, his free hand coming up to press her closer and tangle in her hair before he forced himself to ease back. He appreciated that, at two, their daughter still enjoyed her parents' affection, but he wasn't stupid. In a few short years such displays would be "gross" and they would have to learn entirely new tactics. That was the life they'd asked for. The life he'd yearned for, for so long.

Zeno lifted Nova off his shoulder and set her on her feet, ruffled her already mussed hair, and said, "Why don't you help Mommy out and go wash those hands before we eat?"

Nova sighed dramatically. "Okay." Then she sprinted off for the first-floor powder room.

Harmony traced a finger over his chest. "Is everything settled?"

"Of course." Zeno wrapped his arms around her and lowered his head, letting his lips graze the fully healed mark on the base of her neck. She wore his ring every day, she'd taken his name, but this was the mark that mattered most—to both of them. "My dove," he whispered against her skin. "I do not thank you enough."

Harmony tugged up his shirt until she could press her hands to his skin, a soft, muffled laugh rising from her. "You spoil me rotten. What could I possibly need to be thanked for?"

He kissed her neck, then her jaw, and brushed another kiss to her lips. "Existing, and accepting me." He kissed her again. "You were worth every day of waiting, of searching. You are everything to me."

Tears built in front of her widened eyes, just for a moment, before her smile broadened and she burrowed closer. Her hands spread over his skin. "I love you, too." She squeezed, then eased back, a teasing scowl on her lips. "Now stop making me all mushy, you promised me at least a year of seeing the world before I had to contend with morning sickness again."

Zeno grinned, dropped both his hands to her luscious ass, and kissed her deeply. "So I did." She was fucking perfect for him. He'd endure another four hundred years of solitude if he knew for certain she waited at the end. Her, and the beautiful future they built together.

The End

VOLUME TWO

EVERNIGHT PUBLISHING ®

www.evernightpublishing.com